STOP THE PRESSES!

ALSO BY ROBERT GOLDSBOROUGH

NERO WOLFE MYSTERIES

Murder in E Minor
Death on Deadline
The Bloodied Ivy
The Last Coincidence
Fade to Black
Silver Spire
The Missing Chapter
Archie Meets Nero Wolfe
Murder in the Ball Park
Archie in the Crosshairs
Murder, Stage Left
The Battered Badge
Death of an Art Collector
Archie Goes Home

SNAP MALEK MYSTERIES

Three Strikes You're Dead
Shadow of the Bomb
A Death in Pilsen
A President in Peril
Terror at the Fair

STOP THE PRESSES!

A Nero Wolfe Mystery

Robert Goldsborough

MYSTERIOUSPRESS.COM

NEW YORK

Author photo by Colleen Berg

978-1-5040-2357-3

Published in 2016 by MysteriousPress.com/Open Road Integrated Media, Inc.
180 Maiden Lane
New York, NY 10038
www.mysteriouspress.com
www.openroadmedia.com

To the memory of Rex Stout,

who redefined the detective story

STOP THE PRESSES!

CHAPTER 1

I had just finished one of Fritz Brenner's hearty breakfasts—freshly squeezed orange juice, shirred eggs, Georgia ham, and hash brown potatoes—and gotten settled at my desk in the office when the phone squawked. "Nero Wolfe's office, Archie Goodwin speaking," I answered, as I always did.

"Nice to know you are on the job. It is a real comfort to me." The voice on the other end belonged to Lon Cohen of the *New York Gazette*, newspaperman par excellence and also poker player par excellence, as I have learned much to my chagrin over the years.

"To what do I owe the honor of this call, O Noble Chronicler of the Great City's Foibles, Farces, and Fancies?"

"Flattery will get you everywhere with me," Cohen said. "I have a matter I would like to talk over with your boss."

"Really? Care to tell me about it?"

"I would prefer to discuss it with both of you, and face-to-face. I can come over at Mr. Wolfe's convenience."

"What about at dinner? As you know, Nero Wolfe enjoys your company at the table, and I seem to recall that you enjoy not only Fritz's world-class meals, but also that cognac that he has been known to offer up to special guests, a title for which you qualify."

"I wasn't angling for a dinner, Archie. This could be a daytime visit."

"Understood. I will talk to Mr. Wolfe at eleven, when he descends from communing with his orchids up in the plant rooms, but as I am a betting man, I will lay odds—long odds—that he suggests that you come for dinner."

"Okay, but make sure he knows I am not, repeat *not*, asking for a meal."

I promised Lon I would relay his comment and then turned to finishing the correspondence Wolfe had dictated the day before, most of it letters to orchid growers. I had just typed the last of them when the whirring of the elevator announced that the morning séance in the greenhouse up on the roof was over.

"Good morning, Archie. Did you sleep well?" Wolfe said predictably as he strode into the office and placed a raceme of orange orchids in the vase on his desk.

"Yes, sir, like a baby. It must mean I don't have any guilty feelings lurking deep within my subconscious."

That drew a frown but no comment as he lowered himself into the reinforced desk chair, built to support his seventh of a ton, and rang for beer. I waited until he had signed all of the correspondence and swiveled to face him. "Lon Cohen has requested an audience," I said.

Wolfe's eyebrows rose. "Has he? For what purpose?"

"He didn't say. Just that he had something he wanted to discuss with you, and for that matter, with me as well."

"Just so. Have him come to dinner."

"He said he did not want you to think he was angling to get a meal invitation."

"Nonsense! Mr. Cohen is always welcome at the table here. You know that. There are few individuals with whom I would rather dine. See if he can come tonight. Tell him we are having Capon Souvaroff. I recall that he had it here once previously and spoke highly of it."

"I will do my very best to talk him into joining us this evening."

"I have every confidence you will be successful," Wolfe said dryly as he popped the cap off the first of two bottles of beer Fritz had just brought in along with a pilsner glass.

I was successful. When I called Lon during Wolfe's afternoon visit to his orchids and told him he was invited to dinner, he groaned. "Dammit, Archie, that was not my intent and you know it."

"So I told Mr. Wolfe, but he insisted. In fact, he said some very nice things about you as a dinner guest, things I am not about to share. You've got a big enough head as it is."

"Thanks a heap for putting things in perspective."

"My pleasure. For the record, Fritz will be serving Capon Souvaroff, and the dessert is raspberries in sherry cream."

"Be still my heart," Lon cracked. "See you later."

I have never known Lon Cohen to be late for anything, especially one of Fritz Brenner's meals, and that evening was no exception. At ten minutes to seven, he stepped in out of the blustery February night and took off his overcoat, which I hung on the hall rack along with his homburg.

A few words here about Lon. He has been employed by the *Gazette* for as long as Wolfe and I have known him, which is a lot of years. Early on, he was a crime reporter, and by all accounts, a damned good one. Then he moved to the city desk, and for at least two decades now, he has occupied an office on the twentieth floor, two doors down from the publisher. He doesn't have a title I am aware of, but he wields a lot of clout on the fifth-largest newspaper in America. And he has an encyclopedic knowledge of our city's history and the characters who have shaped it.

Lon also dresses better than anyone I know, which is saying a lot, because both Wolfe and I take pride in our appearance. Our favorite newspaperman favors custom-tailored three-piece suits, white shirts with cufflinks, silk ties, and shoes that have a shine any marine would envy. He wears clothes well in part because he doesn't have an ounce of fat on his five-foot-nine frame, and his black hair sees a barber every other week. His brown eyes, set deep in a tan face, are always alert, always looking for the next big story to splash across the front page.

"Glad you could remember the way," I told him as we walked down the hall to the dining room, where Wolfe already was in the process of getting seated.

"Mr. Cohen," Wolfe said, nodding slightly by way of a greeting. "What do you know about the War of the Roses?"

So our dinner subject had been set. Wolfe never discusses cases during meals, which wasn't a problem tonight as we didn't have a case. But even without a case, he enjoys talking about anything from politics to polygamy. One of his current books was about the War of the Roses, which took place in England hundreds of years ago. I knew next to nothing about it, but Lon did, so the conversation was two-sided, with me listening, learning, and enjoying yet another of Fritz Brenner's three-star meals.

After dinner, we retired to the office, Wolfe and I behind our desks with beer and scotch, respectively, and Lon in the red leather chair at the end of Wolfe's desk sipping Remisier brandy from a snifter.

"As usual, the dinner was superb and the discussion stimulating," Lon said, savoring the Remisier. "I feel guilty taking your hospitality and then presenting you with a problem that doesn't figure to end up with you getting a case."

"Mr. Cohen, we have helped each other on numerous occasions over the years. You have supplied us with valuable information, and we have been able to help present you with newsworthy stories."

Lon laughed. "Help? You have singularly presented the *Gazette* with stories, invariably exclusives, and always wrapped up neatly, like a welcome gift."

The creases in Wolfe's cheeks deepened—his version of a smile. "Would you say that our accounts are more or less even?"

"More or less, with a tilt in your favor, I concede," Lon said, raising his brandy snifter in salute.

"Perhaps a slight tilt. You have the floor. As you know, Archie and I are good listeners."

Lon cleared his throat. "I'm sure the name Cameron Clay is familiar to both of you."

Wolfe pursed his lips. "Your vituperative, confrontational, and sometimes libelous, columnist."

That got a tight smile from Lon. "All of the above and more, although he has rarely been sued."

"He still comes across like a twenty-four karat jerk," I put in. "He throws insults around as casually as a hash-house cook flips burgers. I'm surprised your editors see fit to put him on page three every day."

"You wouldn't be surprised if you saw our readership figures," Lon said. "Clay's Stop the Presses! column is far and away the most popular element in the *Gazette*, year after year."

"I find that hard to believe," I said.

"I don't," Wolfe demurred. "I agree, at least this once, with H. L. Mencken, who said years ago that 'No one ever went broke underestimating the intelligence of the American people.' That is not to say, Mr. Cohen, that many among your readers are lackwits, but they, like so many of their fellow citizens, relish nothing more than hearing half-truths, rumors, salacious gossip, and outright insulting descriptions of those in possession of fame and power. I confess to having read Mr. Clay's column on occasion, but each time I do, I curse myself for having wasted the time."

"We are in basic agreement," Lon said, holding up a palm. "I am no fan of Stop the Presses! myself. To me, the shame is that, although Clay can be a bulldog at ferreting out interesting and sometimes significant information, in recent years he has become ever more intent upon slurring the reputations of civic and government figures and celebrities, whether or not there is any substance behind his accusations and innuendos."

"Your newspaper has a legal department," Wolfe said. "Do not Mr. Clay's printed shenanigans raise red flags with them?"

"Only to a degree. First off, most of those Clay attacks are public figures who, because of their high visibility, have essentially forfeited any claim to an invasion of privacy. And as to libel, the other possible transgression, most of these individuals prefer to avoid the spectacle of a trial. Second, you will, of course, remember the Haverhill family, which has owned the newspaper for decades."

Wolfe nodded. He—and I—had cause to remember that family from a previous case in which the Haverhills, with

Wolfe's help, had to fight to keep the *Gazette* out of the hands of a Scottish press baron whose papers appeal to the lowest common denominator.*

"The Haverhills are very protective of Clay," Lon continued. "Part of the reason, so our publisher tells me, is that Felicia, wife of the clan's current paterfamilias, Eric Haverhill, is an avid reader of the column. So avid that in two libel cases brought against Clay over the years, she has put up her own money to settle both out of court, probably in the neighborhood of a hundred grand."

"A truly loyal reader," I said. "Mark me down as impressed."

"Don't be, Archie. For Felicia, the dough she put up in these cases amounted to no more than petty cash for her. And Eric Haverhill didn't seem to mind. He is in the habit of indulging his wife."

Wolfe took a sip of his beer and dabbed his lips with a handkerchief. "Mr. Cohen, as you stated a few moments ago, we are in basic agreement in our assessment of your well-read columnist's character and behavior in print. I sense you have more to say on the subject."

Lon nodded grimly. "I do. Someone seems bent upon killing Cameron Clay."

---

* *Death on Deadline*, Robert Goldsborough, 1987.

CHAPTER 2

A pause of several seconds followed, not because either of us was surprised at Lon's statement, but because we were *not* surprised. Wolfe broke the silence.

"I would have thought a death threat against Mr. Clay was hardly an unusual occurrence."

"You are right, of course. He has gotten lots of them over the years," Lon said, waving a hand dismissively. "But most are obviously crank calls or scrawled notes, the latter from what we refer to as our 'crayon-wielding readers.'"

"What makes these threats different?" I asked.

"Clay told me it is because of their increasing frequency and similarity, suggesting—at least to him—that they all are coming from the same individual."

"He came to you with this information?"

"Yes. For some reason, he seems to feel that I'm a supporter of his, even though I've never gone out of my way to be complimentary about his work."

"What form have these threats taken?" Wolfe asked.

"They have all been phone calls, most to the office, but some to his home," Lon said. "The voice has always been the same, muffled and probably male, Clay told me. The calls started three or four weeks ago. They are always short, because the caller does not want to be traced, obviously. They usually begin with something theatrical like 'Your days are numbered' or 'Enjoy your time in the limelight while you can, because it is soon to end.'"

"How concerned is Mr. Clay about these calls?"

"I believe they have really gotten to him," Lon said. "In the past, he has always shrugged off attacks, whether by phone or in print. But now he seems damned concerned, although he doesn't want to show it, lest it damage the swaggering 'tough guy' image he likes to project."

Wolfe paused to drink beer, then set the glass down and once again dabbed his lips with a handkerchief. "Is the man given to bouts of paranoia?"

"I wouldn't say so, although maybe that what-the-hell attitude of his is a cover-up for insecurities I'm not aware of. That sounds like cheap psychology, though, doesn't it?"

"Perhaps," Wolfe said. "Did Mr. Clay have any suggestions as to who might be making these calls?"

"I asked, of course, and he listed five individuals he feels bear him the most animosity."

"Only five?" I put in. "I would have thought he could compile a list that would compete with the Manhattan white pages."

Lon's response was a chuckle. "Good point. Lord knows Cameron's collected enemies over the years the way some people collect stamps or coins or Christmas plates. Having said that, I was able to pin him down to naming those who top his 'most hated' list."

Wolfe dipped his chin a quarter of an inch, the signal for Lon to start naming names.

"Several of these probably will be familiar to both of you," Lon said after refilling his snifter with Remisier. "Here they are, in no particular order. Cameron did not rank them with regards to their levels of hatred for him. I'll start with Kerwin Andrews, the well-known builder and developer."

"Some would add 'con artist without equal' to his adjectives," I said.

Lon nodded. "Cameron has called him far worse in his columns, referring to him, although not by name, as 'that too-well-known poseur who possesses the poorest taste since the Edsel.' He described Andrews City, that huge housing development in Long Island City, as 'a monument to the egomaniacal dreams of a charlatan.' He characterized Andrews Tower, the office skyscraper he built in Connecticut, as 'New England's ultimate phallic symbol.' He called the sprawling Andrews Plaza Shopping Center in New Jersey 'that sad, grotesque faux Disneyland on the banks of the Passaic.' He has also suggested that Andrews has 'greased the palms'—that's the term he used—of legislators in the tristate area to get his various projects built, and damn the zoning laws that got violated in the process."

"I seem to recall reading in the pages of the *Gazette* and the *Times* that Mr. Andrews sued your columnist," Wolfe said.

"He did—twice—and lost both times," Lon answered. "Truth is, one possible defense in a libel case, and the *Gazette*'s lawyers were able to prove that Andrews did indeed lavish 'gifts' on state legislators and local officials. Two of these so-called public servants, one each in Jersey and Connecticut, resigned from office before they were thrown out."

"Andrews has plenty of reason to wish Cameron Clay ill," I observed.

Lon nodded. "That's putting it mildly. Andrews didn't take the attacks lying down. He has said on more than one occasion that 'Cameron Clay is the single worst thing wrong with American journalism today.'"

"Childish drivel on both sides," Wolfe snorted.

"I am not about to defend our star columnist," Lon said, "but he does relish getting under the skin of the people he attacks. He loves baiting them, daring them to sue him."

"And, of course, the *Gazette* just happens to relish all of that publicity," I commented.

"True. The editors do little, if anything, to discourage Cameron Clay from being an attack dog. They figure any suits that result are part of the cost of doing business, and I tend to agree."

"The capitalist system at work," Wolfe remarked. "Continue."

At this point, I interrupt the narrative to address a question that had occurred to me and perhaps to you as well: Why was Wolfe giving so much time to this Cameron Clay business? No crime had been committed, we had no prospect for a commission that I could see, and the man who signs my checks clearly has no use for the *Gazette*'s "star" columnist. When I asked about it after Lon's departure, he said, "You will agree that Mr. Cohen is a good friend and a valued source. If he felt concerned enough to discuss this with me, then I owed it to him to hear him out and give such advice as I could. This I have done."

Back to the conversation. Lon then introduced the second among the five individuals Cameron Clay suspected as being behind the threatening calls—Captain "Iron Mike" Tobin.

"The disgraced former cop," I said.

"The selfsame," Lon said. "As you both will, of course, recall, Tobin went to prison for beating suspects to wring confessions out of them. Cameron was the first to write about him when word of his brutality began to leak out. At one time or another, he referred to Tobin as 'a disgrace to the force' and 'the biggest single reason why so many New Yorkers hate cops.' Eventually, the other papers started picking up the drumbeat, and the district attorney had no choice but to weigh in."

"Mr. Tobin ended up spending several years in prison," Wolfe said, "and he was recently paroled."

"That was about six months ago." Lon nodded. "And when he did get out of the slammer after serving three years of a five-year sentence, Cameron wrote that he should have been put away for life."

"Tough talk," I said.

"Yeah, and apparently Tobin did some pretty tough talking himself when he was residing with the state. Other prisoners said he had told them he would 'get that column-scribbling son of a bitch' if it's the last thing he did."

"How has the former police officer kept himself occupied since his release?" Wolfe asked.

"He and his wife live in an apartment up in Yonkers, where he works part-time in a florist shop run by an old friend. Cameron Clay still hammers away at him though, claiming that little job he's got is just for show, that he doesn't really need the money because of all the bribes he got from brothel owners whose establishments he protected—and patronized—when he was on the force."

"Is there any truth to that charge?"

"There always were rumors that, in addition to his brutality, Tobin was on the take from a variety of, well, *entrepreneurs*,"

Lon said, "although nothing was ever proved; it was all hearsay."

"Mr. Cohen, how would you characterize the police department's opinion of Michael Tobin today?"

That drew a smile from the newspaperman. "A damned good question. Officially, the department decries and abhors Tobin's actions and reiterates its strong stance against the use of force in the questioning of suspects. However, if you happened to be in a saloon drinking with a bunch of beat coppers and asked what they thought of Tobin, you'd get a far different response."

"Such as 'we need more like him'?"

"Right, Archie. In fact, one of our reporters, who did not identify himself as such, went into a bar where a lot of police hang out and brought up the Tobin case. The members of the force he talked to said that, in general, they're against strong-arm tactics, but almost all of them allowed as to how people like Tobin are sometimes necessary. 'Too damned many bleeding hearts out there protecting the perps, and some of those bleeding hearts are on the newspapers' is how one patrolman expressed it."

"So it's fair to say that Cameron Clay would not win a popularity contest if everyone in the New York City Police Department had a vote?" I asked.

"No question about it. We've received letters from at least two dozen cops, most of them unsigned and most purporting to be from the rank and file, complaining about Cameron and charging that he's 'anti-police.' We haven't heard from higher-ranking officers, who tend to be much more diplomatic—or should I say *political*?"

"The higher the station of an individual within any organization, the greater the tendency to hew to the company line," Wolfe said.

"It would be interesting to know how your old friend Inspector Cramer feels about Tobin," Lon said. "Not that I am about to ask him."

"Nor am I," Wolfe said. "Who is next on your list?"

"His eminence, City Councilman Millard Beardsley of Harlem."

I laughed. "He's the one who organized that protest march and sit-in at the *Gazette* building last year."

It was Lon's turn to laugh. "Beardsley claims it was a spontaneous event organized by his constituents to protest the way Cameron Clay had treated the councilman in his columns. But, of course, it was general knowledge that Beardsley himself orchestrated the circus."

"Just how has your columnist treated Mr. Beardsley?" Wolfe asked.

"He's been pretty rough on the guy," Lon said. "He invariably refers to Beardsley as 'New York's worst councilman' and he has written that 'one of the great mysteries in our town's long and checkered history is how the man keeps getting reelected.' Oh, and he also noted that 'It's only fitting that Beardsley has the same name as Millard Fillmore, our nation's most forgettable president.'"

"Has Mr. Beardsley indeed done a poor job as a local legislator?"

"I would say that his record has been mixed at best. As Cameron has often pointed out, he has the worst attendance record—by far—on the council. And it has long been an open secret around town that Beardsley has taken money under the table from constituents who want favors ranging from getting zoning variations to getting their property taxes reduced. Cameron likes to refer to him in print as 'Millard "My Palms Are Open" Beardsley.'

"On the other hand, Beardsley does fight for his constituents, much more so than any other councilman I can think of. But Cameron never touches on that, so he has hardly been even-handed."

Wolfe scowled. "Has Mr. Beardsley ever brought suit against either the columnist or the *Gazette*?"

"No, but he did excoriate Cameron in a City Council meeting some months back, referring to him as 'Mr. Cameron "Screw the Blacks" Clay.'"

"Do you see Mr. Beardsley as being capable of doing physical harm to Mr. Clay?" Wolfe asked.

"I would say it's unlikely," Lon said. "Although, given the councilman's alleged ties to organized crime, he could certainly put out a contract on Cameron Clay and keep his own hands clean."

Wolfe made another face. "Proceed."

"Next up in the I Hate Cameron Clay Club is one Roswell Stokes, Esq., lawyer to the disreputable," Lon said. "Or 'Defense Lawyer Unmatched,' as one local magazine headlined a fawning profile on him."

"I don't read Clay's column very often," I said, "but I do recall him dubbing Stokes 'Mr. Malpractice.'"

"All that and much more," Lon continued. "He has been riding Stokes unmercifully for years, blasting the lawyer's overwrought theatrics and his list of clients, many of whom come from the ranks of the syndicate."

"But he usually wins, right?"

"He's got a good batting average, that's for sure. After one well-publicized case in which he got a mobster off, Cameron wrote that 'Another scoundrel of the first order has escaped the clutches of the law, thanks to some questionable antics from the slickest, sleaziest representative of the bar this city has ever seen. Hats off to Mr. Malpractice and a miscarriage of justice, yet again.'"

"I assume Mr. Stokes has never chosen to initiate a lawsuit against his habitual tormenter," Wolfe said.

"Yeah, he probably figured going up against Cameron Clay and the *Gazette* in court would do him more harm than good," Lon said. "But he has taken a few shots of his own from time to time. In an interview with the *Post* last year, he was quoted as saying, 'This city has one too many newspaper columnists, and something should be done about it. I will leave you to figure out who that individual is.' When the *Post* writer pushed Stokes to get specific, he simply—and pompously—said, 'I rest my case.'"

"Does anyone at the *Gazette* review Mr. Clay's columns before they run?" Wolfe asked Lon.

"They go through the copy desk, of course, and I get carbons as well, which I go over. But the desk is under orders not to change anything of substance unless they get a specific directive from the managing editor or from me."

"Do either of you ever order a change or a deletion?"

"Almost never. Our editor and publisher—he holds both titles—issued a memo several years ago saying that the columns should run as written unless a factual error has been found."

"And Mr. Clay does not make so-called 'factual' errors?"

Lon chuckled. "Not technically. He's accurate with specifics—dates, times, and so on. The names he calls people—*nincompoop* and *knucklehead* come to mind—don't qualify as inaccuracies."

Wolfe drained the second of his beers and exhaled a bushel of air. "I believe you have one more name to bring to us."

"And you are going to love this one. It is Cameron's ex-wife—his third ex-wife to be precise—Serena Sanchez."

That brought a scowl from Wolfe. He hates nothing more than cases involving what he terms "rancorous domestic relations." Not that we had a case here, but the very idea of feuding spouses was enough to make him grimace, and this was definitely a situation involving feuding spouses. But even Wolfe, who rarely deigns to read Cameron Clay's column, had to know about the very public split between Clay and his latest ex-wife, the temperamental Spanish mezzo-soprano Serena Sanchez. It had been trumpeted in every paper in town, often with the two of them glaring at each other at some dinner or other public function.

"Are you going to tell me this woman threatened Mr. Clay?" Wolfe demanded, glowering at Lon Cohen.

"That is exactly what I am going to tell you. I'm not sure what you know about this woman, but she is known as the 'Valencian Volcano' because of her . . . well, her explosive nature. You know how it is with opera singers."

Wolfe did not know, and did not care. He has no use whatever for music, which he calls "a vestige of barbarism."

When Lon got no reaction from Wolfe, he plowed on. "Okay, here's the background: A few years ago, Cameron Clay and Serena Sanchez met at a reception following a Metropolitan Opera performance of *Carmen*, which has long been Serena's signature role. For some strange reason, the two of them seemed to hit it off instantly, call it chemistry, if you will, although alcohol may have had something to do with the attraction. Anyway, she had recently been divorced from her husband, an Italian shipping tycoon, while Cameron Clay and his second wife, a foreign correspondent for the *Baltimore Sun*, recently had split up.

"The two became enamored with each other right there

at the reception, it was the damnedest thing, or so people who were present told me. They couldn't keep their eyes—or hands—off each other. They were married six weeks later."

"Disgusting."

"Granted, and also ill-advised. Their marriage was a train wreck from the beginning. She found him uncouth and wedded to his job, which he certainly is, and he quickly realized that her theatrical actions were not an aberration, but rather her everyday behavior. She caused scenes in restaurants and hotels, chewing out waiters, desk clerks, and bellhops."

"I seem to recall that a columnist on one of the other papers said her actions made the recently deceased Maria Callas look like a gentle pussycat by comparison," I said.

Lon nodded. "That certainly was true. In recent years, Serena Sanchez has become the diva to end all divas. And when the couple split after only a few months, their ensuing hatred for each other became legendary. After their mutually agreed-upon divorce, Cameron has often peppered his columns with snide remarks about Serena, things like, 'Gentlemen, do not—repeat do not—marry a diva, whatever else you do. I'm living proof. After a short time being wed to one, I aged ten years,' and 'I see a minimally talented opera singer will be performing at the Met this fall; that's one production you might consider taking a pass on.'"

"That's called playing hardball," I said.

"Yes, Archie, but I'll have to say that Serena Sanchez gave as good as she got. A year or so after their split, when she arrived at JFK to sing at the Met, she was greeted by members of the New York press and TV corps. Not surprisingly, Cameron Clay was not among them. She answered all their questions politely, then asked one question of her own. 'Is that guttersnipe columnist still employed by one of your newspapers?'

"That quote didn't make it on the TV news clips or the other papers, although one columnist for a tabloid—who just happened to be a heated rival of Cameron's—gleefully picked up the quote verbatim, following it with his own words: 'Now who in the world could Miss Sanchez be talking about?'

"Now, if I may be so presumptuous as to anticipate your question," Lon said to Wolfe, "I think Serena Sanchez is quite capable of doing harm to her former husband. Case in point: In one of their frequent public scenes, this in a midtown eatery of some note, she shouted 'I will kill you!'"

"A meaningless outburst from a woman given to histrionics," Wolfe said with a flip of the palm.

"All right then, try this on for size: Years ago in Madrid, the diva shot a man who she said was stalking her. He was wounded, but recovered, and because he had such a shady past vis-à-vis women, the Spanish court did not charge her."

Wolfe's face made it clear that he was disgusted with Serena Sanchez, so he did what he often does in these situations: He changed the subject.

"Does Mr. Clay do all of his own reporting? And if so, is it primarily by telephone?"

"Oh no, like a lot of columnists, particularly ones whose stock-in-trade is gossip and exclusive news tips, he always uses a 'legman.'"

Seeing Wolfe's expression of puzzlement, I cut in. "A legman is usually a young reporter, one commonly referred to as a 'cub,'" I said. "He—or sometimes she—chases down leads, rumors, and so on. Do I have that right?" I asked, turning to Lon.

"Essentially, yes. That is not to say Cameron doesn't have a lot of pipelines, he does. They can be public relations men, cops, taxi drivers, city hall functionaries, even grifters. And he, like other columnists, has been known to pay for juicy tips about who's sleeping with whom and why a certain local businessman no longer resides in the family abode on the Upper East Side."

Wolfe buzzed for more beer. I didn't know how much more of this seamy stuff he could take.

"The current legman is a lad of about twenty-five named Larry McNeil, who, if memory serves, came to the *Gazette* straight out of Columbia," Lon went on. "Normally, these young reporters work for Cameron for one or two years and then go on to city desk assignments, either with us or other papers in town or elsewhere.

"Larry is something of an exception as he's been on the job for a little over three years. Cameron has said, 'He's the best of the bunch, and I've had a lot of good ones. If anything ever happened to me, he could take over and the readers would hardly notice the difference. Now that's saying something, because I am a true original.'"

"Mr. Clay does not suffer from false modesty," Wolfe observed.

"We've got plenty of big egos on the paper," Lon said, "but his is probably the biggest of them all. I know that I have imposed upon you tonight with all of this Cameron Clay business, but I have yet another favor to ask of you."

Wolfe raised his eyebrows but said nothing.

"I would like you to see Cameron Clay and determine whether he has reason to fear for his safety."

"Has he reported these threats to the police?"

"I suggested that course of action to him, but he was adamant against it. He said, 'Hell, the way the cops feel about me, they wouldn't give me the time of day.'"

"Mr. Cohen, I don't know what help I could possibly be,"

Wolfe said. "If one individual is determined to kill another, virtually nothing can be done to prevent the act."

Lon nodded. "You are right, of course. But in talking to him, maybe you can figure out whether there is a basis for his fears."

"Why would he talk to me?"

"Because he has respect for you. When he turned thumbs-down on the idea of reporting the threats to the police, he said, 'What about your private-eye friend? I'd be interested to know what he thinks of all this. Maybe he could see me.'"

Wolfe took a deep breath. He hates to work, and he particularly hates to work when there is nothing financial to be gained from the effort. On the other hand, his respect for Lon Cohen is second only to his respect for Saul Panzer, a freelance operative we often use and a poker player who is even better than Lon. Wolfe was in a pickle, and I was interested to see how he would get out of it.

"It has been a long evening," Wolfe said, rising. "I must excuse myself. You will hear from me or from Archie tomorrow. Good night."

After he left the office, Lon turned to me. "Well, what do you think?"

I shrugged. "I don't have a good track record at predicting my boss's actions, but I can tell you this: Our bank balance is reasonably healthy because of an embezzlement case Wolfe just solved for a good-size accounting firm, so that is on the negative side of the ledger. But Wolfe likes you and always has, so that's on the positive side.

"Back on the negative side is his distaste for work, especially when there is no pot of gold at the rainbow's end, and that trumps any positives. In other words, your guess is as good as mine."

"Thanks for nothing," Lon said. "Wait—what am I saying?

Tonight, I've had a better meal than I could get almost anywhere else in the world, to say nothing of a cognac fit for the gods, and stimulating conversation to boot. Shame on me for complaining."

"I couldn't have said it any better myself, old friend. Go home, get a good night's sleep, and awaken to see what the new day brings."

CHAPTER 3

When I turned in that night, I had absolutely no idea what Wolfe's answer would be. Part of me did not want to get involved with Cameron Clay in any way. The guy obviously was a jerk, and he would almost surely get under Wolfe's skin. My boss is hard enough to live with in the best of times, but with somebody like Clay in the brownstone, he would be more cantankerous than ever.

The next morning after breakfast, I sat at my desk balancing the checkbook, pleased with the numbers. We were in better shape than we had been in some time, thanks to that aforementioned case in which Wolfe—with my assistance—nailed a too-greedy-for-his-own-good accountant.

I figured that alone might be sufficient for Wolfe to give Lon a thumbs-down. When we've got a healthy bank balance, my boss likes to sit back and do nothing more than to enjoy the fruits of his labors—i.e., reading books three at a time, perusing orchid catalogs, doing Sunday *Times* crossword puzzles, and meddling in the kitchen, where he will often argue with Fritz over the ingredients to be used in a specific dish, such as whether to put onions in a shad roe casserole. Fritz is for, Wolfe against.

When Wolfe came down from the plant rooms at eleven, I decided to say nothing about Lon's request. The ball was in his court. He wished me a good morning, rang for beer, and perused that morning's *New York Times* for the next twenty minutes as I entered orchid germination records on file cards.

I was determined not to break the silence, and it turned out that I didn't have to.

"Archie, please get Mr. Cohen on the telephone."

I dialed a number I knew by heart and stayed on the line. Wolfe picked up his receiver, and Lon answered on the first ring.

"Mr. Cohen, this is Nero Wolfe. I will see your Mr. Clay, but with this caveat: I do not possess the resources to prevent one individual from doing violence to another. If Mr. Clay truly fears for his life, I can suggest precautions he can take to minimize the danger to him, but I can do little else. He must understand that."

"That's all he can ask for, Mr. Wolfe. I will pass your message along to him, and I assume he will call you."

"How are you going to stand having that man in the house?" I asked after we had hung up.

"We have had far worse, as you are aware."

"Agreed, but those were situations where we had a case and a client, with the promise of a payment. Here we have nothing, zilch."

"Archie, I applaud your concern regarding our finances," Wolfe said, leaning back and interlacing his hands over his middle mound. "It is admirable, and I commend you. I agree that we have 'zilch,' to use your colorful term, but we also have a long and fruitful relationship with Mr. Cohen."

"But you said yourself when he was here that if anything, the balance is tipped slightly in our favor."

"I prefer to keep it that way. I would always rather have someone in my debt than the reverse."

"Even if it means putting up with a sleaze like Cameron Clay?"

"*Zilch*? *Sleaze*? Your vocabulary has taken flights of fancy. You must introduce me to your dictionary."

"All right, mock me if it gives you satisfaction, but you have been known to use many words that are unfamiliar to most of the rest of us poor mortals."

Wolfe rang for beer and swiveled to face me. "Call Saul and find out if he has the time to do some research on Mr. Clay—his family, habits, anything else he is able to unearth."

Saul Panzer is an operative, but that tag hardly does him justice. He is the best freelance detective on this or any other continent, which is why Wolfe uses him so often and trusts him "further than might be thought credible." He is better at tailing someone than any breed of bloodhound, and he can find out more about an individual than the best spy in the pay of any government in the world.

At 5' 7" and 140 pounds, Saul isn't much to look at, but you underestimate him at your peril. He has more business than he can handle, but he has been known to interrupt a case he's working on at the drop of a hat to give Nero Wolfe a hand. I dialed his number and got Coral, the woman who currently runs the answering service Saul uses.

"Aye, Mr. Goodwin, I recognize your voice," she said in her

pleasant Scottish burr. "May I have Mr. Panzer ring you when he is able? I know that he will check in with me soon."

I answered in the affirmative and hung up, turning to my copy of the *Gazette*'s early edition. It was time to tackle a task I had been avoiding: reading Cameron Clay's column.

As I noted earlier, I am not a regular reader of Clay's work, but I considered this "homework," so I flipped to page three, where the column occupied its usual position at the top of the page, under elaborate Old English type proclaiming "Stop the Presses!" along with a woodcut of what appeared to be an antique printing press. The column carried no other headline, but rather started right in with bold-faced items:

> **NAUGHTY, NAUGHTY**: What Yankee outfielder has been seen on numerous occasions of late at the Stork Club and the 21 Club with a lady (if that's the right word) who most definitely is not his long-time missus? Guess you could call her a pinch-hitter, eh? Stay tuned for updates. . . . **WHEELS UP**: Hizzoner the Mayor has become something of a jet-setter this winter. He tells us trips to Florida, Arizona, and California have been essential to persuade companies headquartered in those states to relocate to Our Town. Does he ever fly to those places in July and August? And does he ever fly to Minnesota or Maine? Just asking. . . . **BROADWAY BOMB**: Word is that a certain musical that recently opened here with a star-studded cast, hysterical hype, and stratospheric ticket prices is on the brink of closing. Nobody associated with this dud is talking, but if we were you, we'd avoid making advance bookings. . . . **VILLAGE VIPERS**: Seems that a number of bars, restaurants, and other establish-

ments in Greenwich Village have been getting visits from city inspectors looking for electrical and other code violations. We're told that for certain "considerations" from the merchants, these inspectors suddenly lose interest and disappear. . . . **"CERTAIN PEOPLE" NEED NOT APPLY**: What hoity-toity Park Avenue co-op tower has quietly decided to ensure that its residents are racially and ethnically "pure"? Word is that one well-known entertainer was turned away when he tried to purchase an available unit because he was deemed "not suitable" by the board. City officials we reached claim to know nothing about this nasty bit of intolerance.

There was more, but I stopped reading at that point, having digested all I could handle in one sitting. To give Clay his due, however, today's column, like many of his others, was not entirely scandal-mongering. He did point out injustices and questionable practices, and I recalled that a few years ago, he was given an award by a neighborhood association for crusading to successfully get a park purged of the drug dealers who gathered there after dark.

As I put the paper aside, the phone rang. "Reporting as requested," Saul said, and I motioned to Wolfe to pick up his receiver.

"Good morning, Saul," he said. "Are you available for an assignment?"

"At your service, as usual."

"I am interested in what you can find out about Cameron Clay, his habits, his foibles, his family."

"Ah, the columnist who fashions himself as 'Mr. New York.' When do you need information?"

"Whenever it is convenient for you. Do not discommode yourself." In Wolfe's eyes, Saul Panzer can do no wrong.

"I'll have something later today," Saul said.

"Only if it does not disrupt your schedule," Wolfe said, hanging up. I stayed on the line long enough to tell Saul that, heaven forbid, we certainly did not want to do any disrupting of his precious schedule. The answer I got was a snort, then a click, followed by the dial tone.

I wasn't so sure we would hear from Saul that day, but as has so often been the case, I underestimated him. The call came at four thirty. "Okay, Archie, I've got some dope on the self-important columnist. When do you want me to unload it?"

"Can you be here at six?"

Saul said he could, which I told Wolfe when he came down from the plant rooms. "Good," he said as he rang for beer.

The doorbell announced Saul's arrival as Wolfe settled into his desk chair. "Apparently, you were not discommoded," I said as Saul stepped in and hung his hat and coat on the hall rack.

"Being around Mr. Wolfe all these years has certainly improved your vocabulary—that is, if you even know what the words you like to throw around mean," Saul said as he ambled down the hall to Wolfe's office. I tried to mount a comeback, but Saul was already settling into the red leather chair.

"Something to drink?" Wolfe asked.

"I'd like a scotch on the rocks, if it doesn't discommode Archie too much," he said.

The creases in Wolfe's cheeks deepened as I went to the kitchen for ice and then got Saul his drink from the serving cart against the office wall.

He took a sip and nodded his approval of the single malt.

"I've got some stuff on Clay, although I'm sorry it isn't more complete."

Wolfe nodded, the signal for Saul to continue.

If Saul wondered why Wolfe had solicited him rather than Lon Cohen for information about Clay, he did not question it. Although Wolfe had said nothing to me, I knew the reason: He felt Lon might be too close to the subject, and he knew Saul had sources outside the staff of the *Gazette*.

"I don't know why you need to know about Cameron Clay, and I am not about to ask," Saul said. "For starters, I can tell you this: It is not hard to find people around town who have an opinion about the columnist, and most of these opinions are less than flattering. This despite the fact that Stop the Presses! is almost surely the single most read feature in any New York newspaper."

"It is not necessary for one to like the messenger to absorb the message he delivers," Wolfe said.

"I suppose not. So it's probable that a lot of people read his column despite what they think of him," Saul replied. "From what I've learned, he gets plenty of mail at the *Gazette*, and it's pretty evenly split between pro and con. But once, a few years back, the editors decided to keep the column out of the paper for several days to test the reaction. And did they ever get one. There were hundreds of calls and letters wondering where Stop the Presses! was. Needless to say, it got reinstated, and Clay himself got a raise out of it."

"Papers have pulled the same stunt with comic strips," I added.

"Probably with similar results," Saul said. "Anyway, here's what I've come up with about Clay. I'm afraid it may not be that helpful, although I'm unsure as to what you hope to learn."

"As Archie likes to say, we are all ears," Wolfe said, finishing the beer in his pilsner glass.

"Okay, here goes. He's sixty-eight and has had his *Gazette* column for seventeen years. Going back to the beginning, he grew up in Maryland, where his father was a foreman at the big Bethlehem Steel plant in Sparrow's Point near Baltimore and his mother was a seamstress who took in work at home. He graduated with a journalism degree from the University of Maryland, became a cub reporter at the *Pittsburgh Post-Gazette*, and later became a police reporter there. There didn't seem to be any other opportunities for him to grow at the paper, so he took a job as a criminal courts reporter at the *Baltimore Sun*. He broke a couple of big stories, and after much pushing and nagging on his part, he was given a twice-weekly column. Within a few weeks, he told the editors he deserved a daily column, but he was turned down—more than once.

"Frustrated, he decided his future was in New York, nothing less would do. He began peppering a half-dozen of Manhattan's dailies with clippings and applications. After months of futility, an editor at the *Gazette* hired him as a general assignment reporter. Clay first made his name at the paper with a piece exposing a crooked landlord who owned a number of tenements and was bribing city inspectors to overlook code violations in his sub-par buildings. He followed up with several other exposés of shady and illegal business practices and outright scams, and as he had done in Baltimore, he began lobbying for a column, although it took him years to get it. He's always been personally aggressive—bordering on the obnoxious—according to my contacts."

"Bordering? The obnoxious part sure comes through in his columns," I said.

"No question," Saul said. "Clay doesn't want to win any popularity contests, quite the contrary. Given what I've learned from a couple of people who know him, he seems to relish riling people up and bringing attacks upon himself."

"The *Gazette* is willing to put up with attacks on Mr. Clay because of his high readership," Wolfe stated.

Saul nodded. "Absolutely, and other papers in town have tried to lure him away. A friend of mine at the *Daily News* told me—off the record, of course—that they once tried to sign Clay to a fat contract, but the *Gazette* raised his salary to keep him. Since then, the *News* has tried three different columnists as competition to him, but none of them has had Clay's sources or his flamboyant writing style."

"Is that what you call it . . . *flamboyant*?" I asked.

"That's what my *Daily News* friend calls it," Saul said. "I've also learned that a lot of people around town are afraid of Clay because he can be mean and vindictive. For instance, if a competing columnist runs an exclusive item about some local celebrity getting divorced or a high-visibility executive switching jobs, Clay finds out who the source of the item was, perhaps a press agent, and tells that individual that 'no item I get from you will ever run in this column again.' That can be damaging to anyone trying to get information about a client into print because Clay's column is a so-called 'must read' when compared to any column in any competing paper."

"A journalistic reign of terror," Wolfe observed.

"Yeah, although from what I also hear," Saul said, "Clay has begun to lose some of his old feistiness, which may be because of his health. It seems he doesn't take good care of himself, never has, and it's begun to catch up with him. He's overweight, and he's both a heavy smoker and a heavy drinker. Somebody I know who has seen him at various functions around town tells me he doesn't look good: pasty-faced, slow-moving, somewhat lethargic."

"The wages of sin," Wolfe said.

"True. And his personal life hasn't exactly been smooth-sailing, with three short-lived marriages, three divorces."

"One of them to that Spanish opera singer," I put in.

"That was the third wife," Saul said. "The first was a college classmate at Maryland and a cheerleader for the football team. They were married for about two years, but it was a bad fit for both of them from the start, and she ended up marrying a former football star at the school.

"Wife number two was a coworker of his on the staff of the *Baltimore Sun*. This union was even shorter than the first, a year and a half. The woman, who was one of the paper's best reporters, was named a foreign correspondent not long after they were married, and she got assigned to Paris. She wanted Clay to move there with her and he said no. They had a trans-atlantic marriage for a short while, but Clay said to hell with it and divorced her. Or maybe she initiated the proceedings.

"Then there was that Spanish opera singer you mentioned, Archie, and that also did not last long. They constantly fought and she, like the second wife, was out of the country much of the time. But that probably didn't matter, as they both had such independent personalities that they were always at each other's throats when they were together."

"Clearly, he isn't cut out to be the marrying kind," I said, stating the obvious.

"And Clay's been very open about that in print," Saul replied, reaching into his shirt pocket and pulling out a sheet of paper, smoothing it on his lap. "Here's something he wrote in his column some years back that I came across: 'I've been married three times: to a cheerleader who never outgrew being "Sally Coed"; to a reporter who expected me to follow her around the world; and to an opera singer whose favorite person in the whole world is herself. Three strikes and I've quit the marrying game. If anyone out there ever learns that I'm thinking about getting hitched again, please call me immediately and do everything you can to talk me out of it. If there is an organization called "Husbands Anonymous," I want to join.' "

"At least he finally learned something about himself," I commented.

"That he did," Saul agreed, turning toward Wolfe. "One other thing: Apparently, Clay has no close friends, none at all. My sources seem to think that's by choice, that he just doesn't like getting close to people. I'm afraid that's all I've got. Sorry I couldn't come up with something more substantial."

"On the contrary, your performance is admirable, especially in so short a time," Wolfe said, handing him a check. "I salute you on your resources. And at some point, Archie and I will share with you the reason for our interest in Cameron Clay. However, now is not the moment."

That was good enough for Saul, who rose to leave, saying he had a date with some pasteboards. "You know, I do have other poker games besides our Thursday night session," he told me.

I was aware that he did, and I told him I felt only pity for those poor saps who would be up against him tonight. "At least leave them enough for cab fare home," I said.

CHAPTER 4

The man is a wonder, isn't he?" I said to Wolfe after Saul had departed.

"Indeed. He goes about his work quietly and efficiently, but he never is satisfied with his performance. He always feels he can do better."

"I don't know how he could have learned any more than he did about Cameron Clay given the short time he had the assignment. By the way, so that I can keep our records straight, what amount did you fill in on that blank check I gave you that was made out to Saul?"

"One hundred fifty," Wolfe said. "Do you take issue with the figure?"

"Not in the least. What's next, Boss?"

He hates it when I call him that, but he ignored the jibe. "Confound it, I suppose we shall have to see Mr. Clay."

"Why? He is hardly the kind of man you—or I—have any

use at all for. As we both are aware, one of my roles in this job is to goad you into working, but here I am talking you out of a case. But then, it really isn't a case, is it? We have no client, no potential fee, no nothing. Zilch, to use that word again. What is to be gained by seeing Clay? Given the kind of person we know him to be, he will only rile you up."

He raised his eyebrows. "And you as well, Archie?"

I threw up my hands. "Yeah, I admit it, me as well. Look, I like and admire Lon Cohen as much as you do. He's a straight shooter and a damned good newspaperman, but how much do we really owe him regarding that irascible columnist of his? Or am I using *irascible* incorrectly? I know how you love to correct my usage."

"To my surprise, you have selected an apt adjective for Mr. Clay, based on what we have learned about the man. However, Mr. Cohen has requested our help, and you will concede that we have gone to him for help and information numerous times through the years."

"We've been over this already—both our relationship with Lon and who's ahead on balance."

Wolfe had heard enough from me. "Archie, call Mr. Cohen and tell him we will see Cameron Clay."

I know when I've lost a battle, so I dialed Lon's number and got him on the second ring as Wolfe picked up his receiver. "Mr. Wolfe is prepared to meet your ace columnist," I said. "Tell him to call here so we can set up a time."

"Hmm. I thought he might already have phoned you."

"Perhaps Mr. Clay has changed his mind about wishing to see me," Wolfe said.

"Could be, but I doubt it. I'll mention it to him again."

Lon's prodding of the columnist must have been effective, because a half hour later, the phone rang and I answered with "Nero Wolfe's office, Archie Goodwin speaking."

"Yeah, this is . . . this is Cameron Clay," came a raspy voice across the wire. "I would like to make an . . . an appointment with Nero Wolfe. Can you set that up?"

"Yes, I can set up an appointment, Mr. Clay," I said, turning to Wolfe for his reaction. He silently mouthed, *Tonight, nine.*

"Would tonight at nine be convenient?" I asked our caller.

"That . . . that's short notice," Clay said with a cough. "But . . . yeah, what the hell, why not, yeah. Here's the location I got from Lon Cohen. Is it correct?" He read off our address.

I told him he had it right, and that we would be expecting him at nine. He coughed again, muttered something like "I'll be there," and signed off.

"Well, the great columnist will be gracing us with his presence," I said. "But do not expect a glib conversationalist. The man seems to stumble over his words. Maybe he's only articulate when he's at the keyboard."

Wolfe grunted, which could have meant most anything, and I didn't bother to question him. He already was grumpy at the prospect of having a visitor he considered to be less than admirable, but I had little sympathy for my boss at the moment. After all, this meeting was his idea, not mine.

CHAPTER 5

After a dinner of braised wild turkey, we were back in the office with coffee. I was catching up on the sports scores in the *Gazette*, while Wolfe had his nose buried in one of his current books, *Roots: The Saga of an American Family* by Alex Haley. The doorbell rang, and I noted that my wristwatch read exactly nine o'clock.

"Well, he gets positive marks for being on time," I said, rising and walking down the hall to the front door.

Viewed through the one-way glass, Cameron Clay did not offer much to look at: *Rumpled* would be my adjective of choice. He wore a battered trench coat, unbuttoned despite the biting winter wind, and his badly knotted woolen plaid tie was flapping in the gusts. His misshapen felt hat looked to be just off the racks of a thrift shop. And while he was by no means in Nero Wolfe's league in the girth department, he had to be carrying no less than seventy-five extra pounds.

"Come in out of the cold," I said with a smile, swinging open the door.

"Thanks," he gruffed as he stepped in. "You're Goodwin, huh?"

"Guilty. Let me hang up your coat and hat, Mr. Clay."

"Cohen tells me that you're a good egg. Surprised I've never had occasion to write about you and your boss. God knows that you both have had your share of publicity over the years."

"Just lucky, I guess," I said as I led him down the hall to the office. He both wheezed and limped slightly.

"Cameron Clay, Nero Wolfe," I said, steering our guest to the red leather chair. Clay must have been prepped by Lon, because he did not hold out a paw to shake hands.

"Mr. Clay, may I offer you something to drink?" Wolfe said. "I'm about to have beer."

"Beer sounds good, and just a bottle. I don't need a glass," he said, adjusting his bulk. He pulled a pack of cigarettes from the breast pocket of his flannel shirt, but looking around, he saw no ashtray and put the pack away, frowning.

After Fritz brought in the beer, two bottles and a chilled glass for Wolfe and a bottle for Clay, the columnist coughed and said, "I guess you know all about why I'm here, right?"

"Mr. Cohen has given us some background, but I would like to hear it in your own words."

Clay nodded, running a hand through thin, graying hair that probably never saw a comb. "As I'm sure you and Goodwin here are aware, I've made my share of enemies over the years, and frankly, I don't give a good goddamn whether people like me or not, never have, never will."

"You must have been threatened in the past," Wolfe said.

"Hell, yes, I have," Clay said, waving the comment away

with a beefy hand. "But most of those were whiny mopes or the rantings of yahoos who were a few cards short of a full deck."

"But I gather you have taken these more recent threats seriously."

Clay shifted in his chair and coughed again. "Yeah, I have. Somebody sounds like they're really serious this time."

"These warnings all have been delivered by telephone?"

"Every one of them, some on my line in the office, some at home."

"Can you give us their essence?"

Clay drank from his bottle and set it down, suppressing a belch. "I'm pretty sure it was the same voice every time, but I think it was disguised because it was sort of fuzzy, like the connection was bad, you know? Maybe the caller had something over mouthpiece, like they do in detective stories."

I wondered what detective stories Clay had been reading, but I held my tongue. I was the silent observer here.

"Was the content of each call essentially the same?" Wolfe asked.

"Pretty much, yeah. Let's see . . . One time the voice—and I am assuming it's always the same voice—said, 'Time's running out on you, and the countdown has begun.' And another time it was, 'Enjoy the spotlight now, because soon, very soon, it's going to be turned off for good.' And yet another time, the words were: 'Good thing you've got no family to mourn you.'"

"What makes you feel these calls should be taken seriously?"

"I can tell you that in the past, people who complained to and about me, either through the mail or on the telephone, invariably mentioned a specific item or subject I had written about," Clay said. "I would be accused of being a 'cop hater' or 'anti-black' because of something negative I wrote about the police or a person of color. These calls refer to nothing specific, and that has never happened to me before."

"Have you engaged the caller in conversation?"

"I have tried to, but each time, I get hung up on before I can get a full sentence out."

"Has any attempt been made to trace these?"

"Hell, that would be totally useless," Clay said with a sneer. "None of the calls ever takes more than a minute, if even that. Also, at least twice I've heard street noise in the background, which means that the person is in a phone booth and would be long gone before anybody could get to the scene."

"Mr. Cohen mentioned that you are loath to involve the police."

"Damned right, that's because they, uh, *loathe* me," he said with a dry cackle, pleased with his wordplay. "If anything were to happen to me, the commissioner would declare a departmental holiday to celebrate. I've been pretty hard on some of the cops, as you know."

"I believe you are exaggerating the institutional animosity toward you," Wolfe said.

"Nah, I don't think so. In any case, uh, I'm not about to go to them. Do you have some suggestions? I'm told you're the best there is, and, uh, I've read plenty about you and your feats in the *Gazette* and all the other rags over the years."

Wolfe ignored the patronizing comment. "Do you live in a building that has security?"

"Only what I've had put in myself. I've owned the same brownstone in Chelsea for—what?—fifteen, maybe, uh, sixteen years now, and I'm not about to give it up. In fact, from the outside it's not all that different from the place you've got here, although somewhat smaller and not nearly as elaborate," he said, looking around the office.

"So anyone bent upon doing you harm would have very little trouble reaching you."

"Well for one thing, I've got this sophisticated alarm system wired throughout the place—God knows I paid plenty for it. For another, uh, I'm not out on the streets in Chelsea a lot. A cab picks me up every morning at ten at my place, and uh, takes me to the *Gazette*. Then at night, the same cabbie drives me to my door, usually around eight, unless I'm going out to cover something. When that's the case, I work out the time and place to be picked up by the same cabbie. I've used him for years."

"So then, your job necessitates your attending numerous functions around the city, such as theater openings, receptions, and other activities?" Wolfe asked.

"Yeah, although not nearly as much as in years past," Clay said between coughs. "I now have the best legman who's ever worked for me, Larry McNeil. He goes to a lot of places I used to, including crime scenes and trials and City Council meetings. He's a damned good reporter, and since he's been with me, he has developed a whole new batch of sources. I just don't get out as much as I used to."

Wolfe drank beer and set his glass down. "Mr. Cohen mentioned five people who you feel are particularly antagonistic toward you."

"*Antagonistic*—a good word, has a lot of punch, I like it," Clay said, clapping his hands. "Yeah, Lon pinned me down to name what I like to call 'the big five.' Oh, there's lots of others who would like nothing better than to read my obituary, but this handful are in a league by themselves."

"Tell us about them," Wolfe said.

Clay held up his empty bottle, peering at it, and Wolfe looked at me. I got the message and went to the kitchen for another beer for our guest. When I returned to the office, he was just starting in. ". . . so I really let the dirty cop have it in print. The bastard had been beating confessions out of suspects, guilty or otherwise, for years."

Wolfe turned to me as I placed a fresh beer on the small table next to the red leather chair. "Archie, Mr. Clay has just begun to tell me about the policeman who was sent to prison for abusing suspects."

"Captain 'Iron Mike' Tobin," I said.

"Precisely. I am sorry to interrupt, please continue," Wolfe said.

"Tobin detests me, hates my guts," Clay said. "But that's okay, I hate his guts, too, and anything I wrote that helped put him away gives me a warm feeling. My only regret is that he got such a short sentence, but then, the judge in the case didn't want to alienate the police, so he went soft on the bastard."

"Mr. Tobin was released from prison a few months ago," Wolfe said. "Do you feel it is a coincidence that soon after his release you began getting these telephone threats?"

"The timing isn't lost on me," Clay said. "I can't say that the voice I heard in the calls is his because of its, uh, muffled nature. But hell, he could be getting someone else to do the telephoning. He's got all sorts of cop friends who probably hate me as much as he does."

"Would you place him at the top of your list of bugbears?"

Clay shrugged. "Hell, maybe. Of the five names I trotted out for Cohen, Tobin's the only one who I helped send to stir. Several of the others on that list should be behind bars as well, but the fact they're still at large is through no fault of mine."

"Let us now talk about those others, sir," Wolfe said. "Where would you like to start?"

"How about that super shyster Roswell Stokes, who Shakespeare must have had in mind when he wrote, 'The first thing we do, let's kill all the lawyers.'"

"*Henry VI, Part II*," Wolfe said. "Do you think Mr. Stokes merits such punishment?"

Clay sniffed. "Oh, maybe not, but he does deserve to be disbarred, as I've written more than once. The man is a disgrace to his profession, and I'm not by a long shot the only one who feels that way. He's been reprimanded by the bar association more than once, and several judges have come down hard on him for his courtroom antics. One even declared a mistrial because of his performance."

"Is his behavior worse than that of other defense attorneys?" Wolfe asked.

"No question, there are other frustrated thespians in the legal world who love to perform, but Stokes is far worse than any of those others."

"Has he threatened you?"

Clay laughed—at least I think it was a laugh, although it came out sounding more like someone stifling a sneeze. "If you want to call it threats, yeah. He's taken a few shots at me, but damned ineffectual ones, like 'this city has one too many columnists' and other equally bland comments. Anticipating your next question, he's never sued me, he's afraid to. If we ever got into court, I would unload on him, bringing up every time he's been reprimanded or had a case thrown out because of his cheap theatrics."

"From what you say, it would seem you have nothing to fear from Mr. Stokes," Wolfe observed.

"Not so fast, Mr. Detective. I forgot to mention that Stokes's client list is dominated by mobsters, most of them with names you would instantly recognize. The mouthpiece would never try to get rid of me himself, he'd hire one of his syndicate pals to do the job for him."

"Have you had any indication that this is likely?"

"Only that on occasion of late, I've seen a nondescript sedan driving slowly by my place, and always the same car, at least as near as I can tell."

"Have you noted make, model, or the license plate?" I asked.

"No, the car always comes after dark, and my eyes aren't all that good anymore."

"Do you make a habit of looking out at the street from your residence?" Wolfe asked.

"I do sound sort of, uh, paranoid, don't I?" Clay said with another one of those dry-as-dust laughs. "Guess I must be getting a little jumpy in my old age."

"And you have absolutely no desire to ask the police to patrol your block?"

Clay waved the suggestion away. "We've already been over that. The day I go to the cops for help is the day I . . . Ah, forget it."

I could tell Wolfe was sore about Clay's "Mr. Detective" remark, but surprising to me, he held his anger in and pushed on. "So . . . are there others you feel are possible sources of those telephone threats?"

The columnist nodded, reaching reflexively for the cigarettes in his pocket, then remembering where he was. "As I know Cohen has told you, I've been especially tough on Kerwin Andrews, the self-styled 'developer supreme.'"

"He also mentioned that Mr. Andrews has sued you."

That brought another of those hoarse laughs. "He did, twice! And he lost both times. Hell, he was an idiot to bring me into court. The *Gazette*'s attorney made mincemeat out of him. It was obvious during the trial that Andrews's own lawyer, the poor bastard, didn't even want to be there. He knew the case was weak. And the second trial was even more pathetic than the first."

"Has Mr. Andrews verbally threatened you?"

"He's called me a disgrace to journalism and so on, if that's, uh, a verbal threat."

"Do you have reason to fear physical harm from him?"

"Probably not from him directly, but like Stokes, he's got mob ties. For all I know, that sedan that cruises along my block may be there because of him."

"Then there is that councilman you have excoriated in print."

"Ah yes, Millard Beardsley, the 'Mayor of Harlem,' according to his self-fawning press releases. The Bloodsucker of Harlem would be a more apt title for him, though, the way he puts the financial squeeze on any constituent who needs favors, such as a building permit or a blind eye to plumbing or electrical code violations. He's rumored to be the richest member of the council, although that's hard to prove because so much of his wealth has gone unreported. One thing that can be proven, though, is that he has the worst attendance record on the council."

"Your relationship is one of mutual distaste."

"That's one way of putting it. Whenever I take a shot at him in my column, which is pretty damned often, he cranks out a press release branding me as a bigot."

"How do you publicly react to that accusation?" Wolfe asked.

"I ignore it, of course, because it simply is not true. And I'm not the only one Beardsley has charged with being anti-Negro. He says the same thing about everyone who dares to criticize him. It's become a knee-jerk reflex on his part, and it's effective because it puts his critics on the defensive. Not me, of course, because I have got enough friends among his own people who will defend me. In print, I've attacked racial injustice for years."

"But that did not stop the councilman from organizing a march to the *Gazette* building," Wolfe said.

"Hah! What a farce. That was one bedraggled band he put together, with their handmade signs filled with spelling mistakes. I think he was hoping hundreds would join the march, but he was lucky if there were twenty-five there."

"I understand Mr. Beardsley is reputed to have ties with members of the underworld."

"Reputed, huh? That's putting it delicately," Clay snorted. "Of course he's got mob ties, has had them for years. They work with him to shake down merchants in the community."

"So it is indeed possible that Mr. Beardsley may be the reason that automobile drives through your neighborhood."

"By God, you could be right, you probably are!" Clay said, banging his fist on the arm of the chair. "That hadn't occurred to me." He seemed somehow pleased at the realization.

"I believe you have voiced your concern to Mr. Cohen about another individual," Wolfe said, saving what he considered to be the most unpleasant discussion for last.

"Hah! Dear ex-wife number three, a soon to-be over-the-hill opera singer and the biggest single mistake of my life. We don't want to leave her out."

Wolfe drew in a bushel of air and exhaled slowly. "Serena Sanchez, I believe."

"Correct. You said earlier that my relationship with Millard Beardsley was one of 'mutual distaste.' It's nothing compared to our distaste for each other."

"Strong words."

"Strong feelings," Clay replied. "If I never see that woman again, it will be too soon."

"Do you consider her a legitimate threat to you?" Wolfe asked.

"Well, she certainly hasn't been the one phoning me, but then, the caller likely isn't any one of those others who could be out to get me anyway, but rather a representative. Back to your question: With that temper of hers, she's definitely a threat. You may not know this, but years ago in Spain, she shot a man."

"I have heard something about that," Wolfe said. "What were the circumstances?"

"Some creep was following her around, or so she told me, and she plugged him when he started to grab her one night out on the street. The guy recovered, and she never got charged. The Spanish court gave her a pass—self-defense, they ruled."

"Not an altogether unreasonable ruling."

Clay shrugged. "Maybe. But she has said on occasion, and in public, that she would like to kill me."

"Hyperbole?"

"Once you've, uh, shot somebody, it seems like it would be just that much easier to do it again," Clay said.

"Perhaps," Wolfe replied. "You have been writing your *Gazette* columns for many years now, and—"

"Seventeen, to be exact," Clay smirked, leaning back and crossing his arms over his chest.

"Is it accurate to say that in those seventeen years, you have alienated many people, including the five we have been discussing?"

"Without a doubt," the columnist said, still smirking and clearly pleased with himself.

"After all these years of stirring the emotions and incurring the enmity of many of those mentioned in your columns, why do you think that you are now receiving threats?"

Clay turned both hands palms up. "Who knows? Bear in mind, uh, I've gotten threats before, although admittedly not as pointed as these have been. Maybe it has something to do with that slimy copper Tobin getting out of jail. The calls started coming after his release."

"That would explain Mr. Tobin," Wolfe said, "but not the others."

"Sorry, but I don't have any answer," Clay said. "Do you have any suggestions as to how I can protect myself?"

"You already have rejected one of them," Wolfe replied, "and that is to enlist the police as protectors. You could, of course, hire a private service that provides bodyguards; there are several in the city. Archie?" He turned to me.

"Del Bascomb's agency is as good as any around town, although there are a number of other good ones," I said.

"Mr. Goodwin can provide you with a list. But I must say this, Mr. Clay: If one individual is determined to kill another, there is very little to prevent the occurrence if the perpetrator does not care whether he or she is caught."

"So, uh, that's it?" Clay said, levering himself upright.

"Yes, sir, that's it," Wolfe said.

Cameron Clay shuffled down the hall toward the front door, with me close behind. I took his hat and coat off the rack and handed them to him.

"Somehow, I was expecting more from your boss," he told me as he slipped the coat on. "I've been hearing for years that he's a genius."

"I would agree with that assessment, but he would never claim to be a miracle worker," I said.

Clay nodded grimly. "That's what I need all right, a miracle," he muttered, going out into the cold night.

CHAPTER 6

"Well, what do you think of the great columnist?" I asked as I returned to the office.

Wolfe looked up from his book. "Pah! The man is living in a fool's paradise. He thinks nothing of insulting people daily on the pages of a newspaper that has a circulation in the hundreds of thousands."

"Over a million," I corrected.

"All right, over a million. Yet he seems totally unprepared for someone who apparently threatens him with death, a threat he claims to be taking seriously. What should he expect? The only surprise is that this did not happen to him much sooner."

"Point taken. At the risk of flattering you, I am impressed that you were so patient with this . . . this scandal-monger."

"I agree, Archie, that Mr. Clay is hardly a paragon, and also hardly a journalistic exemplar. Were it not for Mr. Cohen and his request, I would have rejected seeing the man."

"How serious do you think the threat on his life is?"

"I have no way of knowing. Mr. Clay certainly has made enemies of some formidable individuals. Were I to try ranking these five in the order of the danger they pose to his life, I would lead with the disgraced former police officer."

"Tobin."

"Yes. Mr. Clay played a major part in destroying that officer's career, and few things are worse for an individual than to be forced out of a job in disgrace. Although his was a career that should have been terminated, so in one sense, the columnist performed a public service."

"Care to continue with your rankings?" I asked.

"After Captain Tobin, it becomes more problematic," Wolfe said. "Each of the others, with the exception of Miss Sanchez, had pecuniary interests that had been threatened by Mr. Clay's reportage."

"Pecuniary . . . as in money?"

"As in money," Wolfe confirmed. "The livelihoods of Mr. Andrews, Mr. Stokes, and Mr. Beardsley were all potentially imperiled by Mr. Clay's writings in the *Gazette*. Which of them had the most to lose?" He raised his shoulders slightly and let them drop. "Without knowing more about their portfolios, I cannot say, but each certainly would have breathed easier with Mr. Clay out of the picture."

"How do you feel about Serena Sanchez?"

"I was about to pose that question to you, Archie. What are your thoughts about her?"

Years ago, Wolfe got it in his head that I was an expert on women, a species he claims almost total ignorance of. No matter how often I have told him of my own lack of understanding in that area, he continues to insist that I possess knowledge of the secrets of feminine behavior.

"Of course, I have never met the lady, but based on what I have read and heard, she is a firecracker. Taking into consideration that shooting incident in Spain some years ago, I would say that she probably does not have it in her to plan a calculated, thought-out killing. She seems more the mercurial type, the kind who would react in the heat of the moment. I would associate her with a spur-of-the-moment crime of passion."

"Worded in a most dramatic fashion, Archie, but you confirm my initial impression of her."

"Glad I could be of help. But when all is said and done, what did we accomplish tonight?"

"Very little, if anything," Wolfe conceded. "Mr. Clay came to us ostensibly seeking counsel, but he was reluctant to accept any of our suggestions. He flatly refuses to request aid from the police, and I very much doubt that he will follow our advice and hire bodyguards, although with his salary, I am sure he could easily afford the expense. For one whom claims to be under siege, he seems blithely unconcerned about the potential danger he may well be in."

"That struck me as well," I said.

"What did you think of the man's physical condition?" Wolfe asked.

"He certainly does not look to be in fit shape, does he? He probably smokes too much, which may account for his cough, and he almost surely has got a drinking problem, his complexion is that of someone who does not take very good care of himself. I will tell you this: If I were a life-insurance agent, I sure as hell would not issue the guy a policy."

"What I find most troubling is that I am not sure what he expected from us," Wolfe said.

"Maybe he hoped we would invite him to move into the brownstone."

Even though I was trying to be funny, Wolfe shuddered at the prospect of having Clay around. "I feel we have fulfilled our obligation to Mr. Cohen," he said. "Will you call him in the morning and report the substance of our meeting with this controversial columnist?"

I said I would and went up to bed as Wolfe turned back to his book.

CHAPTER 7

The next morning, when I phoned Lon and told him about our session with Clay, he sighed in exasperation. "Dammit, Archie, I'm sorry to have wasted your and Mr. Wolfe's time. I don't know why Clay wanted to see you if he wasn't about to take any action to protect himself. The man is as stubborn as a mule, as you now have seen firsthand."

"Yeah, he is pretty bullheaded, all right. But then, maybe that's one of the traits that make his column the *Gazette*'s most-read feature."

"Maybe so," Lon responded halfheartedly. "I'm going to talk to our editor-publisher about getting some sort of police protection for Cameron, or at least surveillance in his neighborhood."

"Your boy is really going to love that."

"No doubt," Lon said, ringing off.

We heard nothing about or from Cameron Clay for the next

several days, although I did start reading his column more regularly. I still didn't like his surly tone, but I was clearly not his typical reader.

One morning, just after Wolfe had come down from the plant rooms, the doorbell rang and Fritz went to answer it. He came to the office door wearing a frown. "Inspector Cramer is on the stoop, and he looks angry. Should I let him in?" he asked.

I turned to Wolfe, who scowled. "Very well, Archie," he said, which signaled that I was to be the doorkeeper.

"Good morning, Inspector, it's nice to see you on this brisk winter morning," I said, swinging the door open. "It has been a long time since you've graced us with your presence."

"Not long enough," he growled, shunning my offer to hang up his coat and hat and steaming down the hall to the office. He made for the red leather chair without uttering a word and planted himself, chin sticking out. The thickset inspector wore his usual scowl, and his bulk, while not in Wolfe's league, filled the chair.

Wolfe looked at him with raised eyebrows but said nothing.

"I assume that you know why I'm here," Cramer spat.

"I confess that I do not," Wolfe said evenly. "But I suspect you are going to enlighten me."

"You're damn right I am! What's all this about you telling that obnoxious *Gazette* columnist that he should get himself private bodyguards? Why didn't you let us know that he's in danger? Last time I checked, we were the official law enforcement agency in this city. Has there been a change that I'm not aware of?"

"Inspector, I hardly feel it is my place to call the police every time someone comes to me claiming he is imperiled."

"It would have been a courtesy," Cramer fumed, "as if you

know what *courtesy* means. I get this call from your pal Cohen at the *Gazette*, asking that we keep watch on Cameron Clay's brownstone in Chelsea because he's been getting threatening telephone calls. So one of my men goes to see Clay to let him know that his place is under surveillance, and the newshound blows his stack, saying that 'I told that damned Nero Wolfe that I didn't want the police getting involved. Go away!'"

"Mr. Cramer," Wolfe said, ignoring the slur about courtesy, "it is true that Cameron Clay came here seeking my advice as to how to protect himself because of threats he had been receiving. I proposed a private security service only after he had vehemently rejected my first suggestion, which was that he should inform the police about these threats. It appears that he and the department have enmity for each other."

"I am by no means a fan of Clay and his column," the inspector said, "but that would not influence me regarding his protection."

"He has been very hard on the police department in his writings," Wolfe commented.

"Without doubt. I understand from Cohen that one of the five individuals Clay suspects of making those calls is Mike Tobin, which doesn't surprise me in the least. Clay's columns played a big part in Tobin's downfall, and as far as I'm concerned, that was a good thing. I may not like Clay in particular or his columns in general, but off the record, I like Tobin even less—or I should say not at all. He was a cancer in the department, and it would not have bothered me to see him serve a longer sentence than he did.

"What puzzles me, though, is why you spent time counseling Clay," Cramer continued. "He's not a client, is he?"

"He is not," Wolfe replied. "I saw him as a favor to Mr. Cohen.

Now that I have answered your question, I will pose one of my own: Does it appear that someone is stalking Mr. Clay?"

"Not that my men have been able to discover. We know that he claims a sedan has been driving slowly down his street with some frequency, but we haven't seen it."

"It is possible that a police presence on the street has driven the so-called stalker away," Wolfe suggested.

"Maybe. We are using unmarked cars, of course, but we are aware that all of the cars are easily identified by those who make a habit of avoiding the law."

"Perhaps the telephone calls to Mr. Clay are empty threats, meant to cow him, although if that is the desired effect, I doubt it will work," Wolfe said. "He does not appear to be easily cowed."

"I suppose the threats might be serious," Cramer said. "Lord knows, the guy has made enough enemies over the years. And if somebody does get him, all hell will break loose around town, and you know it. I can just see the headlines now, in the *Gazette* as well as in all the other papers: POLICE FAIL TO PREVENT MURDER OF CRUSADING COLUMNIST! or something similar."

"The papers tend to be protective of their own, which is hardly surprising," Wolfe remarked.

"And I am all for a free press," Cramer said, holding up a hand as if taking an oath. "The papers and their reporters can be a real pain in the behind sometimes, but I'm smart enough to know that we need them."

"I agree that they are vital to the fabric of our society, Mr. Cramer. Back to Clay. If anyone is bent upon killing him, as he seems to believe, there is little anyone can do to prevent it unless he agrees to live permanently in isolation and under guard, a highly unlikely occurrence."

"You're right, of course," Cramer muttered. "We can't force him to be cautious; it probably runs against his nature. Well, I'll just prepare for the worst." He got to his feet and went down the hall to the door, with me following in his wake. I bid him a good-bye but got no response as he left the brownstone and went down the steps to a black Ford sedan that idled at the curb.

"Well, as usual the inspector left here an unhappy man," I told Wolfe, "but at least this time you are not the cause of his unhappiness, as is so often the case."

"Mr. Cramer finds himself in a bind," Wolfe said. "A high-profile private citizen claims he is in peril, and now it is on the record that the police are aware of the situation. If something does happen to Mr. Clay, the department will be held accountable."

"But the police can argue that they got no cooperation from Clay in their attempts to protect him," I put in.

"They can and they probably will, but if Mr. Clay is harmed or worse, how effective do you think their argument will be? If the inspector can suggest potential newspaper headlines, so can I, and here is one: LAME POLICE EXCUSE IN DEATH OF COLUMNIST: HE REFUSED OUR AID. As contentious as Mr. Clay has been, the public sympathies would doubtless be overwhelmingly with him in the event of his death, and the department's defense of their actions would be seen as ineffective, if not downright irresponsible."

"You are actually making me feel sorry for Cramer and the department."

"Their position is a difficult one," Wolfe said. "Knowing what I do about Mr. Clay, I would not be surprised to learn that he is enjoying the department's discomfort."

"Maybe so, but I can't imagine that Clay can be enjoying his own discomfort, knowing that someone is out to get him."

Wolfe made no reply, turning to an orchid catalog that had arrived in the morning mail. I knew that he had had enough of Cameron Clay and his predicament, and did not consider it any of his business. That meant we were in total agreement.

CHAPTER 8

That night, Lily Rowan and I went to the Rangers game at Madison Square Garden, followed by a late supper at Rusterman's, the superb Midtown restaurant that had been founded by Wolfe's late and close friend, Marko Vukcic. Lily and I have been an item for a number of years, and if you were to ask me to define "item," I would politely but firmly tell you to mind your own business.

Lily is beautiful, rich, and, as she describes herself, "lazy." I do not totally agree with the lazy part, because for years she has served tirelessly and generously on the boards of organizations that aid orphans, single mothers, and the homeless. She has what I would describe as ash-blond hair, which nicely complements her dark-brown eyes, and she is a head shorter than me. She is a superb dancer, which is why you will find us in the ballroom of the Churchill Hotel on many evenings.

For Lily, home is the lavish, tenth-floor penthouse of a

building on Sixty-Third Street between Madison and Park decorated with paintings by Renoir, Monet, and Matisse, among others. Lily's money comes from her late father, an Irish immigrant who made his fortune by building much of Manhattan's current sewer system. But as rich as Lily is, we need to get one thing straight: Whenever we go out on the town, which is often, I pay. Period.

We met years ago in an unlikely place, a meadow in rural upstate New York. I was working on a case with Wolfe,* and circumstances were such that I was being chased across said meadow by an angry bull. I jumped a fence to avoid its horns and landed unceremoniously on my rear end, although on the safe side of the fence.

My awkward acrobatics were observed by a beautiful young stranger—Lily—who applauded me and said, "Beautiful, Escamillo. Do it again."

I quickly got to know Lily and soon learned from her that Escamillo is a toreador in the opera *Carmen*, the same opera, by the way, in which Serena Sanchez has made her name.

Back to the present: At the end of a fine evening, Lily and I were having coffee and dessert at Rusterman's. The Rangers had come from behind to beat Montreal before a full house at the Garden, and we celebrated the victory with a dinner of one of the restaurant's signature entrées, boned duck à la *rouennaise*.

"You have seemed lost in thought tonight, Escamillo," she said as we finished our coffee. "Have I somehow lost my allure?"

"That will never happen," I told her. "Sorry, but I did not realize I was distracted."

"Aha, all of which means you and Nero Wolfe must be in the

---

* *Some Buried Caesar*, Rex Stout, 1939.

middle of a case," she said, putting a slender, manicured hand on my arm and squeezing it lightly. "I recognize the symptoms."

"Oddly enough, we have no case at present, my love. Just a strange situation, involving a well-known and widely read newspaper columnist."

"Well known, eh?" she said. "Well, this town certainly has several who fall into that category. But, of course, it can't be Walter Winchell, because he's been dead and gone for several years now."

"Try Cameron Clay."

Lily made a face like someone reacting to a bad pun. "Ouch, why would you want to have anything to do with *him*?"

I proceeded to tell her about the recent events involving Clay. She nodded and took on a thoughtful expression. I awaited the words of wisdom that invariably follow one of my discussions of a case, or in this instance, a non-case.

"I met Cameron Clay once, at a reception following the opening of a Broadway musical that lasted only two weeks. He was a boor and at least half-drunk, and came on to me."

"I will at least give him points for having good taste," I said.

"But the lout's pickup lines were both pathetic and crude. It was all I could do to keep from jamming the heel of my pump into his instep. And then there was his breath . . ."

"You never shared that little episode with me."

"I tried to put it out of my mind seconds after it happened," Lily said. "Fortunately, I've never crossed paths with Mr. Clay again, although I have met his former wife, Serena, the opera singer, and I rather like her, although I can't say I know her all that well."

"Tell me about it."

"A few years back, she was at the Metropolitan Opera singing *Carmen*—"

"The one with Escamillo in it."

"Of course, how could either of us ever forget that? Anyway, I met her after one of the performances. Clay wasn't around; they had already divorced. Nevertheless, we hit it off, and I asked if she would consider singing an aria from the opera at a benefit I was hosting for a youth foundation. She did, which helped make the evening a smashing success."

"Do you still keep in touch with her?" I asked.

"Only occasionally, as she sings and teaches all over the world. It's intriguing that you should bring her up now, though. According to an opera-going friend of mine, Serena's been around here for the last couple of months, teaching master classes in voice at Juilliard and at that school down in Philadelphia. She's apparently between opera engagements, although I have heard she is doing far less singing these days."

"Very interesting."

Lily raised her perfect eyebrows. "Ah, when you say 'very interesting,' I get suspicious. Are you going to tell me you think that because she's in town, she could be the one who has been making threatening calls to her loutish ex-husband?"

"If she is, she's got an incredible vocal range, because Clay says his mystery caller has a masculine voice, albeit fuzzy. That's not to say Miss Sanchez couldn't put someone up to making telephone threats for her."

"As I've said, I really don't know her that well, Archie, but I have trouble believing she would want Clay killed, as dreadful as their marriage was."

"She apparently once said, in public, 'I will kill you,' or words to that extent."

"Yes, I remember hearing about that, too, but bear in mind that Serena is known for her volatile temper. She's a hot-blooded Mediterranean, and she probably said that in the heat of the moment."

"She's also got an itchy trigger finger. Years ago, she shot a guy in Spain who had been bothering her."

"I did not know that," Lily said, clearly surprised.

"The man she shot, who had a reputation for bothering women, survived, and she got off without being charged. Apparently, the judge felt she had just cause, or else he was beguiled by her charms. But that event underscores what you refer to as her 'volatile temper.'"

"I'm sure she's done her best to forget the episode."

"But chances are, Cameron Clay hasn't forgotten, because we know he was aware of the incident."

"Which raises the question: How did *you* know about it?"

"I am a crack private investigator. I make it my job to know things about people that they don't want known."

"Well and good, Crack Private Investigator. Would you care to see me home and come up for a nightcap?"

"I thought you would never ask."

CHAPTER 9

For the next several days, I banished Cameron Clay from my mind, hoping that somehow he would go away. But then, one snowy morning, I got a call from Lon Cohen.

"Even though he is not a client, I felt you would be interested in an update on our churlish columnist," he said. "He has flatly refused to accept either a bodyguard or a service, even though the *Gazette* offered to foot the whole bill. He won't talk to the police, either. Commissioner Humbert even called our editor and publisher, Ashton Cordwell, and asked him to force Cameron Clay to sit down with Cramer's men, but Cordwell said he could not make Clay do anything that he didn't want to."

"It would appear that your man has a death wish," I said.

"He is certainly not doing anything to help himself," Lon agreed. "I keep thinking I'm going to get a call at home one night telling me that . . . well, you know."

"I do. But it's possible that whoever is calling Clay just wants to scare the hell out of him, perhaps as revenge for some past insult."

"Maybe you are right," Lon said, sounding unconvinced. I was skeptical, too.

I began reading Stop the Presses! every day, if only to see whether recent events had caused Clay to mellow. But if anything, he had become even more bombastic and controversial, with many of his sharpest jabs aimed squarely at the five people he had claimed the most likely to be threatening him.

Here are a few samples collected over a ten-day period:

> **SPRINGING A LEAK**: The shoddily constructed Andrews Shopping Plaza over in Jersey is back in the news—for the umpteenth time in a negative way. . . . A water pipe in the central atrium burst this week, flooding the halls and causing a shutdown of the entire mall. . . . Only last month, a section of the ceiling collapsed for no apparent reason, causing another closure. . . . As usual, the developer, Kerwin Andrews, was unavailable for comment. . . . Wonder if the people who finance his shopping centers, office buildings, and housing developments will ever get wise to the fact that Andrews's projects are like houses of cards—ready to collapse at any moment.
>
> **MR. MALPRACTICE GETS AROUND**: Roswell Stokes, Esq. (whatever else you do, please don't forget the "Esq.") finds the time in his busy courtroom schedule to unwind in the presence of a comely damsel. . . . Several times recently, the oh-so-natty defense attorney has been seen at chi-chi spots around town in the company of a raven-haired beauty who has more

curves than an Olympic slalom course. . . . We do not yet know this lovely lady's name, but perhaps one of our loyal readers can enlighten us as to her identity.

THE CAPTAIN TAKES HIMSELF A TRIP: Stop the Presses! has just learned that former New York City Police Department Captain Michael "Iron Mike" Tobin—yes, the same man who went to prison for brutalizing suspects—has lately been seen lolling on the sandy beaches of a terribly fashionable Caribbean island. (Hint: it rhymes with "tuba.") . . . This is the same island, you may recall, where New York mobster Aldo Marshall (née: Moretti) has his palatial wintertime retreat. . . . You may also recall that Captain Mike was often seen in the company of Mr. Marshall before his incarceration. . . . It is something of a comfort to learn that old friends may well have been reunited far from our town's frigid clime.

THE DIVA SURFACES: For any of you out there who might have been wondering what has become of the legendary (at least in her own mind) mezzo-soprano, Serena Sanchez, I have news. . . . The diva (full disclosure: She once was briefly my wife, the more's the pity), has quietly returned to our island and is rumored to be teaching a master class in voice at Juilliard. . . . And if that is not enough to fill her time, she also has been known to commute down to Philly to do teaching at their Curtis School of Music. . . . One can only hope she doesn't scream at her students they way she once screamed at her conductors—and also at me.

> **OH, MILLARD, MILLARD:** Our worst councilman has done it again. . . . Millard "My Palms Are Open" Beardsley of Harlem has missed yet another council meeting, his sixth in this session, which may qualify as a record. . . . The reason given, according to his press secretary, is that he was called to the bedside of an elderly friend who had fallen on an icy Harlem sidewalk and broken his hip. . . . Perhaps if Mr. Beardsley would insist that his constituents' sidewalks were better maintained, he might be freed up to attend to the occasional council meeting. . . . It would be refreshing for a change to see him in the august body with his peers. . . We hope the Honorable Mr. Beardsley remembers where his seat is. (Hint: second row, fourth chair from the left as you face the lectern.)

I was intrigued enough with my findings from Clay's columns to put the clippings on Wolfe's desk blotter the next morning. After he had come down from the plant rooms, placed orchids in a vase on his desk, settled himself, and rang for beer, he glanced at my labors.

"What is this?" he demanded, holding up the sheets.

"Items gleaned from the columns of one Cameron Clay over the last several days. I find it interesting that Mr. Clay seems determined to tweak the noses of the people he most suspects of being behind those telephone calls."

Wolfe glowered at me and pushed the clippings away after scanning them. "I have minimal interest in what Mr. Clay chooses to write, although I do salute you for correctly using the word *glean*. One of its definitions is 'to gather information or material bit by bit,' which you have done here."

"I thought you might have found it interesting that Cameron Clay appears to have a death wish."

"I find nothing whatever interesting about that man," Wolfe said, picking up one of his current books and opening it. Seeing that the subject of Cameron Clay was closed, I began entering orchid germination records provided by our orchid nurse, Theodore Horstmann, onto file cards. Wolfe had no use for Cameron Clay, and I was not about to disagree with him. Besides, I was about to leave town and escape the winter, at least temporarily. That very afternoon, Lily Rowan and I would be on a southbound plane from Kennedy Airport. Destination: the Virgin Islands, where we would spend ten days basking in the sun, laying on the sand, and scuba diving, among other diversions. When I had told Wolfe of our plans, he had shuddered—not because I would be away and unavailable, but because to him the idea of anyone willingly boarding an aircraft and traveling at the speed of a bullet while miles above the earth's surface was an act of wanton recklessness.

CHAPTER 10

Our trip to the Caribbean was everything Lily and I could have wished for—perfect weather, gentle breezes, calm seas, wonderful food and drink, and each other's company, something neither of us has ever grown tired of. But as good a getaway as we had, ten days was enough, and I was eager to get back home, even if there was no case to work on.

Our flight home arrived at midnight. The next morning, I realized one thing I had missed in the islands was breakfasts of the quality served up by Fritz Brenner, and I told him so, causing him to blush. Fritz likes to be complimented, but at the same time, it embarrasses him. "I have missed you, Archie," he said as he served me a second helping of poached eggs and Canadian bacon.

"Not as much as I've missed you and your culinary skills," I replied. "Now Miss Rowan and I had some good meals down there in the islands, but nothing that can compare with the masterpieces you dish up here for lunch and dinner every day." That brought another blush.

"I think he misses you, too," Fritz said, referring to Wolfe. "He always seems a little out of sorts when you are away."

"I sincerely doubt that," I told him. "I'm sure he doesn't miss my nagging him to work when we're in the middle of a case or talking to him when he's trying to read a book. I tend to get on his nerves."

"Perhaps, Archie, but I suspect that sometimes he gets on your nerves, as well."

"I won't deny that," I said, laughing. "But still, it's good to be back."

One of the drawbacks of taking a vacation is that, in my absence, the office chores do not magically take care of themselves. When I settled in at my desk with coffee, I found a batch of invoices for books, groceries, meat, and beer neatly stacked on my blotter, along with a subscription renewal form for an orchid publication and instructions from Wolfe as to how to reply to several letters that had arrived in the last week.

I had begun to write checks for the bills when the phone rang. It was Saul Panzer.

"Welcome home. How was the trip?"

"Wonderful. Did you miss me at Thursday's poker game?"

"We sure did, since you are usually a contributor. But everything was topsy-turvy. The big winner was—are you sitting down for this?—Fred Durkin."

"Well, I will be damned." Fred is one of the freelance operatives Wolfe often hires, and he's as brave and honest as they come, but he is neither quick-witted nor particularly adept with the pasteboards and usually leaves our game with his wallet lighter than when he arrived—like me.

"So that's the big news of the week, I gather?"

"Not really, Archie. Have you listened to your radio this morning?" I told him I hadn't.

"Well, if you do happen to turn it on, you will quickly learn that early this morning, in his brownstone, Cameron Clay was found dead of a gunshot wound."

"Now I really will be damned. What's being said about it?"

"Nothing so far. Too early. Apparently, his legman, a kid named McNeil, found the body."

"I'm trying to figure out if I'm surprised or not," I said after taking a deep breath. "As we both know, a healthy number of people around town will be happy to hear the news."

"A very healthy number," Saul agreed.

"I know that you never asked Wolfe—or me—why we were interested in learning more about Clay, and if I were to make an educated guess, I'd say you're eventually going to find out the answer."

"I can wait. When I get an assignment from your boss, he's got a good reason, and that's all I need to know."

"I feel pretty much the same way when I get an order. I guess you could say we are both good soldiers. It's safe to say you'll be hearing more from us about Clay soon."

"You know how to reach me," Saul said, ringing off.

I sat for several minutes mulling whether to call Wolfe in the plant rooms or wait until he came down at eleven. Knowing how much he dislikes being disturbed when he's playing with his posies, I decided the news could wait. Besides, just before I left for the islands, he'd made it clear that he was not the least bit interested in Cameron Clay.

I had almost caught up with my paperwork when Wolfe strode into the office. "Good morning, Archie. I trust you had a pleasant sojourn. You must have arrived home very late last night."

"I did and I did. And it seems that I am back home just in time to hear some interesting news."

Wolfe threw a look my way. He hates it when I am being what he calls 'enigmatic.' "Confound it, report!"

"Yes, sir. This morning, Cameron Clay was found in his home, dead from a gunshot wound."

That earned me a second look, this one wide-eyed, but it did not interrupt him from buzzing for beer.

"Saul telephoned earlier," I said. "He had heard about it on the radio and thought we would like to know."

Wolfe waited until Fritz had delivered the beer and he had taken his first sip of the day before speaking. "Call Mr. Cohen."

"And here I thought you weren't interested in Clay."

"Archie, call Mr. Cohen."

Like a good soldier, I followed orders, dialing as Wolfe picked up his receiver. Lon answered on the first ring, barking "Yeah, what is it?" over the cacophony of yelling voices.

"Archie here; sounds like you've got a hundred people in that office of yours."

"I'm not in my office, I'm in the newsroom. My calls are being routed down here," he yelled. "All hell is breaking loose, as you can imagine."

"Mr. Cohen, this is Nero Wolfe. What details do you have on Mr. Clay's death?"

"Very few at present. He died of a single gunshot wound. His legman, Larry McNeil, found him. The police are initially saying it was a probable suicide," Lon shouted over the noise around him.

"Very well, we will talk later, when it is more convenient for you," Wolfe said, and we hung up.

"And here I thought you weren't in the least interested in

Mr. Cameron Clay," I told him. "That just goes to show how much I know."

Wolfe did not respond to my barb, and I was not in the mood to goad him any further. Besides, I had a feeling something was eating at him, but I'm not smart enough to figure out what it was. I went out onto the stoop and picked up our early edition of the *Gazette*, which had a headline in three-inch capital letters that screamed COLUMNIST CLAY FOUND SHOT DEAD AT HOME! The accompanying story had few details, other than to quote Inspector Lionel T. Cramer as saying, "Indications at this time point to suicide, although we are exploring all other options." He did not say what those options were, but one would have to rule out "accidental death," which left murder.

It turned out that murder was on the minds of the brass at the *Gazette*, as we were soon to learn. Shortly after Wolfe and I had finished lunch and were back in the office, Lon Cohen called. "Sorry that I was so abrupt earlier," he said, "but you can appreciate the chaos in the office at the time."

"I can indeed, Mr. Cohen," said Wolfe, who had picked up his instrument on my signal.

"Our owner and our editor-publisher want to come and see you, Mr. Wolfe."

"To what end?"

"They are not buying the suicide business."

"What is your opinion? You probably knew Mr. Clay better than either of your superiors," Wolfe said.

"I am wrestling with the question myself right now," Lon said. "On the side of murder is the lack of a note. On the side of suicide is Cameron's rapidly declining health."

"When Mr. Clay visited us, he seemed far from healthy. What was the nature of his illness?"

"According to Larry McNeil, he had been diagnosed with lung cancer and had been given a year, two at the outside. He also suffered from diabetes."

"Did Mr. Clay tell anyone else of this cancer diagnosis?"

"Not that I'm aware of. Cameron didn't seem to have any close friends, perhaps by design, with the possible exception of Larry, who shared the news with me. For all I know, he may have been the only person Cameron confided in, at least involving health matters. He never told me how sick he was, although it did not take a genius to realize that he was going downhill. You could see that by looking at the man. I just had no idea how rapid the descent was."

"Why specifically do your owner and your editor want to see me?"

"To hire you. They don't believe Cameron killed himself, despite what the police seem to think. They are absolutely convinced that he was murdered."

That drew a frown. I long ago reconciled with the realization that I will never fully understand Nero Wolfe and how his mind works, but in this instance, I believe I had at least a shred of insight. He had certainly not liked Cameron Clay—that was obvious from their one meeting—but he also seemed fascinated by the man's total disdain for the opinions of others, a trait that he himself possesses in spades.

"Mr. Cohen, these men would undertake certain risks by hiring me. For one, they would have absolutely no control over my findings."

"I told them as much, but they are willing to take their chances and want a meeting with you."

"Very well. I presume they understand that I make it a practice to conduct all of my business here."

"I made them aware of that."

"Have them here at nine tomorrow evening, but with one proviso."

"Which is?" Lon asked.

"That you be present as well."

CHAPTER 11

"Pardon my curiosity," I said to Wolfe after we had ended the call, "but why insist on Lon's being present at tomorrow's meeting? Not that it bothers me in the least."

"It seems clear to me that both the owner and the editor of the *Gazette* have great respect for Mr. Cohen, as well they should. His being in attendance will only increase their respect for him, but far more important to us, he surely knew Cameron Clay better than either of his superiors, and he may well be able to contribute to the discussion."

The next day's *Times* and *Gazette* each had more details on Clay's death. According to the front-page articles in each paper, the columnist was found at about eight in the morning by his legman, Larry McNeil, who said that he went to Clay's home every weekday morning to map out the day's assignments.

That night, the front doorbell rang at five minutes to nine.

After noting the trio on the stoop through the one-way glass, I opened the door with a smile.

I had never seen the pair who entered with Lon. The taller of the two introduced himself as Ashton Cordwell, the editor and publisher of the *Gazette*. He cut a dashing figure at six feet two inches, lean and with a chiseled profile, razor-cut salt-and-pepper hair, and a three-piece pinstriped navy blue suit that would have been right at home on a model posing in *Gentlemen's Quarterly.* Cordwell looked like the Ivy Leaguer he was, having graduated from Princeton. He gave me a tight-lipped smile as he handed me his black cashmere overcoat and homburg, both of which I hung on the hall rack.

Eric Haverhill was several inches shorter than Cordwell and several pounds heavier, with some of that weight in the double chin under a round face topped by a balding pate. He also was tight-lipped, but without the smile, and he hung his own coat and hat on the rack. He could have taken style tips from either Cordwell or Lon, but perhaps he felt that having a controlling interest in America's fifth-largest newspaper was sufficient to impress people.

In the office, I got them seated, Haverhill in the red leather chair and Cordwell and Lon in the yellow ones. I then reached under Wolfe's desk and pressed the buzzer, his signal to enter from the kitchen, where he had been waiting to make his entry.

"Good evening, gentlemen," he said as he walked in and settled himself behind his desk. "Would you like something to drink? I'm having beer."

"I will take a scotch on the rocks," Haverhill said. "After what's been going on these last two days, I need one."

"I'll second that order," Cordwell said, crossing one leg over the other. "The *Gazette* has been in the center of a media feeding frenzy, with every paper in town banging on our doors to get details on Cameron Clay's life and habits, to say nothing of the wire services and radio and TV networks."

"What the hell, make it three," Lon said.

I went to the kitchen for ice and then returned, moving to the serving bar against the wall to pour their drinks, plus one for me, as Fritz walked in with Wolfe's beers.

"Mr. Wolfe, before we begin," Eric Haverhill said after clearing his throat, "I was just a kid the last time you had occasion to get involved with the *Gazette*, and I want you to know that our family still very much appreciates what you did for us in solving the murder of my grandmother Harriet Haverhill."

Wolfe nodded curtly. He has never been able to handle compliments graciously, but that is not to say he doesn't like to get them. "You and Mr. Cordwell had wished to see me," he said.

"Not just to see you, to hire you," Cordwell said, getting a look from Haverhill that indicated he was to be the spokesman. "The police believe that Cameron Clay committed suicide. We do not. We are absolutely convinced that he was murdered."

"The reason for that conviction?" Wolfe asked.

"First, no suicide note has been found," the editor-publisher said after sampling the scotch and nodding his approval. "Second, he had been getting threatening telephone calls. Third, and most important, Clay was a man of immense self-esteem, some would term it arrogance. In any case, he was hardly the type to destroy himself."

Wolfe readjusted his bulk. "I have found that the police usually have good reasons for their beliefs."

"Hah!" Haverhill snorted, turning again to his chief executive.

"Mr. Wolfe," Cordwell said, "as I'm sure you know, the murder rate in New York City is running well ahead of last year's numbers—and we're less than two months into this year. We, and most of the other papers in town, have written articles and editorials about this alarming trend. Our editors—and I'm sure Lon here will agree—feel that the police will do everything they can to keep the homicide numbers lower, even if it means labeling a murder a suicide."

"I have worked with the police for many years, admittedly with some disagreements, but overall I have found them in general to be honest and thorough in their investigations. I find it difficult to believe they would cover up a murder simply for the sake of statistics," Wolfe said.

"We understand from Lon that you have a long relationship with Inspector Cramer. We do not think it is Cramer who wants to finagle the numbers, but rather some of the higher-ups."

"Specifically Commissioner Humbert," Haverhill cut in. "He is little more than a political hack interested in covering his"—the newspaper owner took a breath before continuing—"his tail, and the latest murder numbers have him back on his heels. The last thing he needs now is the murder of a prominent figure to underscore the gravity of the situation."

"Have either of you shared your dissatisfaction with the police?" Wolfe posed.

"I have," Cordwell said. "In a one-on-one meeting with Humbert yesterday, I told him that we at the *Gazette* felt that the department was not pursuing the cause of Clay's death vigorously enough. He assured me in his dismissive, flip-of-the-hand manner that everything is being done to ensure that Clay's death is thoroughly investigated, and that in his understanding, all indications point strongly to suicide. I felt like I was talking to a wall, so I got up and left."

"As I know you are aware, Mr. Clay came to me to discuss the telephone calls he had been receiving, and I offered some suggestions that he chose not to act upon," Wolfe said. "Well and good, but it seemed clear to me in our relatively brief conversation that he was not in the best of health."

"Admittedly, I only saw him on rare occasions," Cordwell said, "so I'm not aware of any specific problems other than his being overweight. Are you, Lon?"

I've always said that Lon Cohen is one cool customer, and he showed it at that moment. He wrinkled his brow as if in thought. "Well, Cameron had seemed to slow down somewhat in the last few months, but I put that at least in part down to advancing age. And bear in mind that for years, he was tireless and had worked practically around the clock. That can take a lot out of a man."

"I always thought Clay lived a, shall we say, *unconventional* life," Cordwell said. "That never bothered me. He was a unique sort, and it does not surprise me that his lifestyle had aged him."

"He made a great many enemies along the way," Wolfe observed.

"That he did," Eric Haverhill said, "but it is all part of what made him such a draw to our readers."

"I also understand he incurred a number of lawsuits."

Haverhill nodded, smiling. "Yes, but there were fewer than might be expected, given his confrontational style. You should know that my wife, Felicia, was one of his biggest fans, and she ponied up the money—her own money, by the way—to settle a couple of these suits, specifically ones filed by Kerwin Andrews, the developer."

"That was quite generous of her," Wolfe said.

"I suppose. The interesting thing is that Felicia didn't much care for Clay as a person. He is not easy to like, as you probably found out when you met him. But she just delighted in reading the column. I accused her of being a lover of gossip, which she did not deny. But she also was quick to point out that Stop the Presses! was the best-read thing in the paper."

"That is certainly true," Cordwell said, "and it has been at the top of all of our readership studies for the last several years running."

"I have not spoken with the police since Mr. Clay's demise, nor is there any reason I should have," Wolfe said. "Beyond what has been in your paper and those of your competitors, what can you tell me about the circumstances surrounding his death?"

"Well, I'm sure you know from your reading that his body was found by Larry McNeil," Cordwell said. "Larry went to Clay's townhouse each morning around eight for his daily assignments, and he was surprised that the front door was ajar, which was most unusual. He went in and found Clay lying on a living-room sofa with a pistol in his hand and a wound to his right temple. It was clear to Larry that Clay was dead, and he immediately telephoned the police."

"You have stated there was no suicide note," Wolfe said. "As far as you are aware, did the police find anything else in his home that would shed light on his death?"

"I asked Commissioner Humbert that very question," Cordwell replied, "and he said nothing was found to indicate that the death was a murder. Humbert then pointedly added that 'It is a common fallacy that all suicides leave a note.' Mr. Wolfe, I know that your fees are high, but we are willing to compensate you well for finding Cameron Clay's murderer."

"You misunderstand my position," Wolfe said. "I do not accept cases in which any stipulation is placed upon me."

"We have no stipulations," Haverhill insisted.

"Oh, but you do," Wolfe said. "You expect me to identify a murderer."

"Well of course that's what we expect!" Haverhill said. "But we are not specifying who that individual is."

"What if there is no murderer, Mr. Haverhill?"

"I beg your pardon?" the *Gazette* owner said, gaping at Wolfe.

"Let us assume, for the purposes of this discussion, that Mr. Clay did kill himself. What if suicide were to be the result of my findings?"

"That is simply absurd!" Haverhill squawked. "Totally absurd."

"Perhaps," Wolfe said, shrugging. "But I need to make clear that if I am to undertake an investigation, no restrictions can be placed upon me."

"That strikes me as an eminently reasonable position," Cordwell said, turning to Haverhill. "I think we should abide by whatever conclusion Mr. Wolfe comes up with," he added.

"Uh, yes, of course, of course," the *Gazette* owner mumbled, clearly dissatisfied.

Cordwell, who seemed to know how to handle his boss, turned back to Wolfe. "Would fifty thousand dollars be acceptable to you?" he asked.

"Yes," Wolfe said, "plus expenses."

"I assume you would require an advance."

"Yes again. Half now and half upon completion of the assignment."

"Just how do we know it will be completed?" Haverhill asked, still hot under the collar.

"I believe we can set that question aside for now, Eric," Cordwell said soothingly. "Mr. Wolfe has a sterling reputation, as you yourself know from the work he has performed in the past for your family, and to which you alluded earlier."

Haverhill nodded but said nothing. Cordwell pulled a

checkbook and a gold pen from his breast pocket and began writing. "This is drawn on the *Gazette*'s corporate account at the Metropolitan Trust," he said to Wolfe. "Is that agreeable to you?"

"It is," Wolfe said.

"We thank you very much for your time, Mr. Wolfe," Cordwell said, standing as both Haverhill and Lon also rose. "May we request that you keep us posted on any progress, with Mr. Cohen being the conduit? Also, feel free to draw upon him for anything you might need from the *Gazette*. I know you and he have often worked together in the past and we appreciate the close relationship you have."

Wolfe nodded, slipping the check into the center drawer of his desk.

CHAPTER 12

Well, let the games begin," I said to Wolfe upon returning to the office after seeing the *Gazette* trio out. "Haverhill seemed far from happy, Cordwell nodded what seemed like his approval of your position, and Lon winked at me. This should be very interesting. Got any initial instructions?"

"None at the moment."

"I think I see why you *really* wanted Lon to be present. You knew his bosses would want him as the go-between, didn't you?"

Wolfe gave me his version of a smile but said nothing, and I figured he was through thinking about the death of Cameron Clay for now. Knowing that Fritz had turned in, I wished Wolfe a good night and picked up the empty glasses of our guests, along with Wolfe's glass and beer bottles, and took them to the kitchen.

The next morning, after breakfast, I went to the office with coffee and found that Wolfe had left instructions. A handwritten note had been left on my desk blotter.

> *AG*
> *I want to talk first to Mr. Clay's assistant, Larry McNeil. Tonight would be preferable.*
> *NW*

When Wolfe uses *preferable*, he really means *imperative*, as I long ago learned. I dialed Lon's number. "Somehow, I knew it would be you," he said. "What did you think about last night?"

"I was mildly surprised that Wolfe accepted the commission," I told him. "And you?"

"Nothing our two guys said surprised me very much, Archie. As you no doubt could tell, Ashton knows how to deal with Eric, which has been helpful to us on the news side of the paper. Eric has this tendency to meddle in the editorial operations, and Ashton can handle him very well. Our owner knows that his editor is smarter than he is. In fact, Ashton has two Pulitzers from his days as a reporter. They speak loudly."

"I noticed that Cordwell knows how to handle his boss, all right. But having said that, your owner was not exactly happy when he left here last night."

"There's a reason. His wife, Felicia, was absolutely passionate about Clay's column."

"And also about Clay himself?"

"Oh no, no, not at all, which Eric pointed out last night," Lon said. "But she loved reading his stuff, particularly the seamier items, the affairs, divorces, innuendos, insults, political backbiting, all those things that Cameron loved to write about. It is hardly a stretch to say Felicia was his biggest fan. And she is absolutely convinced he was murdered and has been pushing Eric to get to the bottom of it. From what I'm hearing, she's obsessed with nailing a murderer."

"Does she have someone in mind?"

"I'm not sure of that, but she simply cannot believe Clay did himself in."

"So she's pushing her husband. Ah, the power behind the throne. But it seems that Cordwell, who's plenty level-headed, thinks Clay was killed as well."

"Yes, he feels very strongly about it," Lon said. "But I know you called for a reason. What's the plan of attack?"

"My boss wants to talk to Larry McNeil."

"Not surprising. McNeil seems to be pretty broken up right now, and on top of that, the police have given him a thorough grilling, despite their belief that this was suicide. I suppose Wolfe would like to see him soon."

"Good supposition. Tonight, nine o'clock."

"Well, he's in the office this morning helping go through Cameron's files. I'll talk to him and get back to you."

Half an hour later, Lon rang. "Okay, McNeil will be at your place at nine. I hope Wolfe goes easy on him. As I said before, he's shaken."

When Wolfe came down from the plant rooms, I told him Clay's assistant would be here as requested. "Anything else?"

"Not for the moment," he said, placing a raceme of purple orchids in the vase on his desk and ringing for beer. "We may find it instructive to talk to Mr. McNeil."

The young man arrived at the brownstone on time, a point in his favor. Larry McNeil was slim and just shy of my height, with close-cropped blond hair and a long, thin face that wore a somber expression.

"I have heard a lot about Nero Wolfe," he said as I hung

his coat up, "and I've always wanted to meet him, although I'm sorry that it has to be under these circumstances."

"A lot of people meet Mr. Wolfe under less than ideal circumstances," I said as I led him down the hall to the office. Wolfe was seated at his desk and greeted our guest with a dip of the chin. "Would you like something to drink?" he asked. "As you see, I am having beer."

"A beer sounds good to me," McNeil said, and I went to the kitchen to get him a bottle and a glass. When I returned, he was in mid-sentence. ". . . so I had just graduated from Columbia, and Cameron—Mr. Clay—took a chance on me, even though my only experience was as a reporter at a small daily over in New Jersey during the summer between my junior and senior years."

"Did Mr. Clay make it a practice to hire assistants with little, if any, experience?" Wolfe asked.

"Yes, he did, sir. He said he wanted to train his legmen himself. 'Most colleges don't train you for the real world,' he told me. 'I learned that myself when I was in school. You will learn everything that you need to know from me.'"

"What were your functions as Mr. Clay's legman?"

"Where to start? For one thing, he assigned me to attend various meetings, the City Council sessions, for example. The *Gazette* has a beat reporter who regularly goes to those meetings; however, my role was not to cover the news but to supply feature stuff, such as which councilmen fell asleep during the meeting or whether Millard Beardsley was in attendance. Mr. Clay loved to tweak Beardsley, which was easy because he missed so many meetings and never said much at the ones he showed up for.

"I also would make the rounds of the best Midtown restaurants to report on which celebrities were there and who they were with. If you read the column, you may remember an item a while back about a Yankee outfielder who was seen around town with a woman who wasn't his wife. That was mine," he said gleefully, "and Cameron loved it. 'That guy's been sleeping around for years,' he told me. 'We really stuck it to him.'"

Wolfe displayed no emotion, but I knew he was appalled. "I recall that the column did not identify the baseball player," he said.

"No, but everybody in town knows who it is," McNeil replied. "I never saw Cameron so happy about an item I came up with."

"Mr. Clay certainly was not averse to making enemies."

McNeil nodded grimly. "Yeah, and it got him killed."

"You found the body," Wolfe said. "Tell us about the circumstances."

"I've already told the police everything, but I realize you want to hear it from me. Each weekday morning, I would go to Cameron's brownstone in Chelsea at eight, and we would plan the day over coffee and the bagels I picked up from a local deli."

"Couldn't you have just as easily made these plans over the telephone?" Wolfe posed.

"Oh sure, but Cameron seemed to enjoy our meetings, and for that matter, so did I. It gave him a chance to talk about what he wanted to put in the next day's column. He used me as a sort of sounding board, and sometimes we would bounce ideas back and forth. Occasionally, he even took my advice."

"Then came that fateful morning."

McNeil exhaled loudly. "Yeah, I got there right around eight, as usual, but I was hungover, and I do mean really hungover. I'd been to a good friend's bachelor party the night before with six other guys in a second-floor party room of a tavern down in the Village, and we didn't break up until after six thirty in the morning."

Wolfe pursed his lips, clearly disgusted. "Did you go straight from there to Mr. Clay's home?"

"I stopped at my place to get cleaned up, then I went to Cameron's. I had my own key to his brownstone, but I didn't need it, because the front door was ajar, which was very unusual."

"I understand Mr. Clay had an alarm system," Wolfe said.

"Yeah, he did, but a lot of times, he'd forget to switch it on before he turned in for the night. He was careless by nature."

"But was he so careless that he would have forgotten to check the front door to make sure it was closed?" I put in.

"I have to admit that I'd never seen it before," McNeil said. "What usually happened was that I would ring the doorbell, and Cameron would disarm the alarm system, then I would use my key to get in. Anyway, I went on in and headed for the living room, where we always met. He was . . . he was sitting on the sofa near the front windows. At first I thought he was dozing, but then I saw that . . . that both his eyes and mouth were open, and that a revolver was lying on the cushion next to him, just below his right hand, which hung limp."

"You established that he was dead?" Wolfe asked.

He nodded, swallowing hard. "I had taken a first-aid course in school, and I knew enough to check his carotid and his pulse. Nothing. It seemed like he'd been dead for a while."

"Was the revolver his?"

"It certainly looked like it. Once a couple of years ago, I asked him if he was worried that somebody might come after him at home, and he grinned and pulled open a drawer in a living-room end table, pulling out the pistol. It sure looked like the same gun he was shot with, but I don't know if the police found another one in the house."

"I noticed that you didn't say 'the one he shot himself with,'" I said. "You don't think it was suicide?"

"Not at all!" Larry McNeil bristled. "Cameron would never, ever kill himself."

"Do you have a candidate as the killer?" Wolfe asked.

McNeil replied to a question with a question. "Are you aware that he had been receiving threatening phone calls lately?"

"Yes," Wolfe said. "Had you been privy to any of those calls?"

McNeil nodded. "Only once. It was on a morning when we were meeting at Cameron's place. He picked up the ringing phone and immediately got angry and red-faced. He said something like 'Who the hell are you?' and then he slammed the receiver down so hard I thought it would break. I asked what the caller said, and he told me it was just somebody trying to scare him. He said he'd gotten several calls like it recently."

"Do you believe Mr. Clay took the threats seriously?"

"That morning, he acted like he wasn't all that concerned, but I knew him well enough to tell that he was shaken."

"Did he say who he suspected was behind the threats?"

"He listed several possibilities, as maybe Mr. Cohen has told you."

"I would like to hear those possibilities from you," Wolfe said. McNeil proceeded to reel off the same five names Lon had mentioned.

"Do you feel any one of them is the likeliest candidate?" Wolfe asked.

"Well . . . based on things that Cameron said to me, both that morning and at other times, I think he felt he had the most to fear from Tobin, that ex-cop and ex-con. But just to be clear, he told me that he could never identify anyone in any of the calls he got. He figured whoever was on the line was disguising his voice."

"That would seem to eliminate Miss Sanchez."

"I suppose," McNeil said, "but then, she might have got someone else to do the phoning."

"I understand Mr. Cameron was having health issues," Wolfe continued.

"Serious ones," McNeil said. "He had diabetes, and he had been diagnosed with lung cancer. He had been to several doctors, and they gave him anywhere from six months to two years."

"That had to have shaken him up," I said.

"Well, Mr. Goodwin, as I've indicated, Cameron always tried to hide his feelings, and that was also the case with his health. He acted, at least with me, like the problem didn't exist. I guess you could say that he was in denial."

"What will happen to the column now?" Wolfe asked.

"That's out of my hands," McNeil said. "Of course, I would love to be considered as a candidate, but my youth and relative inexperience would probably work against me."

"Since you do not believe Mr. Clay took his own life, do you have any theories as to what might have transpired in his home before you arrived on that morning?"

"I don't, and as I told the police, I'm really baffled," McNeil replied. "I have got to assume that Cameron admitted someone after shutting off the alarm, someone who he must have known."

"Because you are operating on the assumption that Mr. Clay was murdered, do you feel the killer was one of the five individuals he is said to have feared most?" Wolfe posed.

"I have no other explanation," McNeil said, throwing up his hands.

"Then, if that were the case, would he have knowingly admitted one of them to his home?"

"I don't have an answer, and it's been gnawing at me. That plus the fact that I found the front door ajar."

"After your morning meetings, did you both go to the *Gazette*'s office?" Wolfe asked.

"Not together. I usually got a cab to the paper right after our meeting. Cameron went in later, usually around ten. He had a standing order to be picked up by the same yellow-cab driver every day, and the same man brought him home at night, unless, of course, he had an evening function to go to."

"The driver's name?"

"Uh, Walter, Walter . . . Bartlett. That's it . . . Bartlett."

"Have you a telephone number for him?"

"I'm sure it's somewhere in Cameron's files in the office. I can get it for you."

Wolfe leaned back in his chair. "Please do, and give it to Mr. Goodwin. Is there anything more you would like to add?"

McNeil shook his head. "If something comes to mind, I will let you know, sir. This must not go down as a suicide."

"I am sure we will be in touch," Wolfe said as I rose from my chair to usher Larry McNeil out.

"Well, what did you think of him?" I asked Wolfe when I got back to the office.

He grunted. "An intelligent young man, and also an ambitious one. We have not seen the last of him."

And Wolfe has accused *me* of being enigmatic.

CHAPTER 13

I had finished typing the letters Wolfe had dictated the day before when he came down from the plant rooms, asked if I had slept well, and settled into his reinforced desk chair. He had just rung for beer when the doorbell rang. Because Fritz was occupied with taking the beer in to Wolfe, I did the honors of going to the front door. Through the one-way glass, I saw the solid figure of Inspector Cramer. He was not smiling.

I returned to the office. "Your old friend from New York's finest," I told Wolfe. "Do I admit him?"

"Confound it, yes."

"Good morning, Inspector," I said, opening the door.

"Just say 'morning,' and I'll tell you whether it's good or not," he growled, not bothering to take off his hat and coat as he marched down the hall to the office.

"So, that business about not having a client in the Clay case was another one of your cute little tricks, eh?" Cramer said, planting himself in the red leather chair as if he owned it. "And to think I actually believed you. When will I ever learn?" He slapped his forehead with the palm of his hand and pulled a cigar out of his breast pocket, jamming it unlit into his mouth.

"Mr. Cramer, when you asked me that question on your last visit, I told you the truth. At that time, I did not have a client."

"So you say," Cramer replied, gnawing on the cigar. "I assume that you are now going to take what clearly was a suicide and magically transform it into a murder, earning yourself thousands of dollars in the process."

"My commission, sir, is to determine the circumstances of Mr. Clay's death, not necessarily to prove that it was a murder."

"As if the police are not skilled enough to do this, right?"

"If you are firm in your conclusions, my involvement should not be a detriment to the department and its work."

"Oh sure. All that your buddy Cohen has to do to cause a ruckus is order up a story in the *Gazette* that says something like, 'Nero Wolfe, the noted private investigator, has been engaged by this newspaper to determine the circumstances of Cameron Clay's death.' See, I even used your own words. Once the hundreds of thousands of readers of the *Gazette* see that, we will be deluged with calls from people demanding to know why we're insisting this was a suicide. And, of course, the other papers will pick the story up and start running editorials about how the department doesn't want another murder on the books."

"What can you do to persuade me it was a suicide?" Wolfe asked, raising his eyebrows.

"For starters, there was no note," Cramer snapped. "Second, Clay's health had deteriorated. The medical examiner said he had an advanced case of lung cancer and probably wouldn't have lasted much more than a year or two. Third, the only fingerprints on the revolver—*his* revolver, we know—were his own. Fourth—am I going too fast for you?—no one was seen or heard entering or leaving Clay's brownstone in the hours before his young assistant, McNeil, arrived for his usual morning meeting with his boss around eight. And five, would Clay have sat calmly on his sofa and let someone shoot him?"

"What time did the medical examiner estimate that Mr. Clay died?" Wolfe asked.

"Sometime between one and four that morning. That's as close as he wanted to pinpoint it."

"All right, let me address your points, sir: One, as we both are aware, not every suicide leaves a note; two, Clay was a man with a formidable ego and probably would have wanted to continue writing his column until the very end; three, a killer could easily have erased his or her prints from the revolver and then pressed Clay's prints on the handle; four, because Clay likely died in the early hours of the morning, both vehicle and foot traffic on the street likely would have been almost nonexistent; five, it is possible that Clay was shot elsewhere in the house, perhaps after having been surprised or even sound asleep in his bed, and then moved to the sofa to make it appear to be a suicide; and six, the front door being ajar suggests that an individual who somehow had gained admittance to the home had left in a hurry."

"All right, Wolfe, my points may have some holes, I grant you that," the inspector said, "but so do yours. For instance, assuming Clay was distraught about his health and had planned to kill himself; he would hardly care whether or not his front door was closed."

"Well taken, sir," Wolfe conceded. "I acknowledge that there are unanswered questions. I assume you are aware that Mr. Clay had received threatening telephone calls."

"Yes, so his assistant has told us, and your buddy Lon Cohen affirmed it when we talked to him, although I wish he had volunteered that information earlier."

"Have you talked to any of those Mr. Clay suspected of harassing him?"

"We have not, because of our belief that this is a suicide. But I suppose you're going to grill them, or have you already?" Cramer said in a belligerent tone.

"Not yet. Mr. Cramer, I assure you it is not my intent to in any way disrupt your department's investigation of Mr. Clay's death."

"That's what you say, although you've done plenty of disrupting in the past. Why should this time be any different?"

"At the risk of being accused of self-aggrandizement, I will point out that on numerous occasions, I—with the help of Mr. Goodwin and others in my employ—have been of assistance to you and the police department, and in most cases have not asked for, nor sought, publicity or acclaim."

"I'll concede your point, although in most, if not all, of those cases, you no doubt received a handsome payday."

"I acknowledge that, sir, and make no apologies. But very often, our goals, yours and mine, are similar. I may have had my differences with your approach or that of your superiors, but I have never *publicly* disparaged the New York City Police Department or the quality of its service and its dedication to the community."

"My God, I feel like standing up and applauding," Cramer said sourly. "Okay, I grant that with a few exceptions I could mention, you've been pretty square with us over the years. Just don't tell Sergeant Stebbins I said that. You know how he feels about both of you."

"You mean good old Purley Stebbins," I chimed in. "Yes,

we have had our moments over time. And I suspect we'll have more of them."

"Well, I've said my piece," Cramer announced, rising.

"Before you go, sir, a question," Wolfe said. "Was Mr. Clay's home searched by the police?"

"Only in a cursory manner, since it was obviously a suicide, whatever you may think. My men did look for a suicide note, but according to the report I got, they were only there for a relatively short time. Don't trouble yourself to see me out," Cramer said to me. "I know the way."

I followed him to the door nonetheless, and closed it behind him as he descended the steps and climbed into a waiting sedan.

"He never even threw his cigar at the wastebasket when he left like he usually does. He actually took it with him," I told Wolfe back in the office. "Do you think he might be mellowing?"

"Unlikely. But he is clearly upset at the prospect that the reason for the death of a well-known local figure is being called into question, and by extension, the work of the department is also being questioned."

"I wonder how Cramer knew you had been hired."

"If I were to venture a conjecture, it would be that Mr. Haverhill is our man."

"Good guess. It's obvious that he doesn't hold any great affection for the police, particularly Commissioner Humbert. He probably leaked word to somebody in the department just to stir things up there. You realize, of course, that now it's just a matter of time before the folks from the press, radio, and TV begin banging on our door or calling—yes, Fritz?"

"Pardon me, but I thought you should know that a truck from one of the television stations has just pulled up outside, and—" Fritz was interrupted by the ringing of the front doorbell.

"As I was saying, it was just a matter of time. I will try to keep the barbarians away from the gates of Rome," I told Wolfe before heading down the hall. Two men, one with a TV camera resting on his shoulder, stood on the stoop. "Sorry, we're not in the market for subscriptions today," I told them. "So—"

"Mr. Goodwin, I am Marty Masterson from TV NewsFirst," the other man said, "and we want to get some quotes from Nero Wolfe about Cameron Clay's death."

"How did you know who I was?"

"Really, Archie Goodwin, modesty does not become you. Everybody knows who you are," Masterson said.

"Flattery gets you no points around here. Mr. Wolfe does not give interviews. End of discussion." I slammed the door.

Masterson pressed the bell a couple of more times, but gave up. Fritz later told me the pair went back down to the street and Masterson talked into a portable microphone while the photographer took shots of him with the brownstone behind him.

Back in the office, I gave Wolfe a summary and then answered the phone in my usual manner.

"Yes, Mr. Goodwin, this is Darryl Stinson of the *Times*. We understand that Nero Wolfe is investigating the death of Cameron Clay, and I would like to talk to him about it."

"Mr. Wolfe is not available for interviews, nor will he be."

"We are well aware that Mr. Wolfe is known to play favorites—specifically the *Gazette*—and we find that highly offensive, given our position."

"I am sorry you feel that way, Mr. Stinson, but as I said, Nero Wolfe simply is not available." He started to say something in an angry tone, but I realized the conversation would go nowhere and hung up.

"Well, it appears the *New York Times* will not be sending you a Christmas card this year," I told Wolfe, who set his book down but said nothing. "I believe we can expect more calls and visits from the folks who cover the news."

"When you speak to Mr. Cohen, inform him of the interest being shown by his newspaper's competitors, both those in print and on the air."

"I will do that. What comes next?"

"Get Saul. I want the two of you to comb through Mr. Clay's residence. You can get a key from Mr. McNeil. After that, I want to meet separately with each of those five individuals Mr. Clay seemed most threatened by."

"That could be a tall order."

"You have handled what you term 'tall orders' in the past. I have no doubt you will be successful."

I could have been either flattered by that comment or angered that Wolfe was patronizing me. I opted for the former and called Lon. "First, you should know that the word is out that we're on the Cameron Clay case. I've been fending off calls and visits from newshounds of both the print and TV species."

"I'm not surprised. Our owner may be responsible for that. But we're keeping the lid on Wolfe's involvement until he has something definitive to report."

"Second, can you ask Larry McNeil for the key to Clay's place? Saul and I are going to give it a thorough once-over."

"He's in here today, helping to clean out Cameron's office. Assuming he's got the key with him, I'll have it messengered over to you."

"Glad to hear that. Now I need another favor. Can you get me phone numbers and addresses for what I like to call the 'Fearsome Five,' that handful of people Clay seemed to fear most?"

"I saw that one coming. Do you happen to have a pencil handy?"

"You know me better than that. Fire away." Lon gave me what I needed to reach each of them, and we rang off.

"Okay, I've got the numbers and addresses we need," I said, swiveling in my chair to face Wolfe. "I await further orders."

"Let us talk after you have been to Mr. Clay's home," Wolfe replied, rising and striding off to the kitchen, presumably to supervise Fritz's lunch preparations.

CHAPTER 14

While Wolfe and I were in the dining room consuming a lunch of sweetbreads amandine in paddy shells and green-corn pudding, the telephone rang twice and the doorbell once. After lunch, Fritz reported that the visitor at the door was a *Daily News* reporter and that the calls were from the local ABC and NBC television stations, each wanting to come here for interviews.

"I was firm but polite with each of them," he said. "I made it clear that Mr. Wolfe was not available, nor was it likely that he would be. The *Daily News* man was most persistent, but I said to him that it is impolite to call upon someone without telephoning first."

"You need to explain that to Inspector Cramer sometime," I said. Fritz gave me a puzzled look, trying to figure out whether I was serious.

"Thank you for shielding us while we were dining," Wolfe said. "Archie will handle all calls and visitors now."

I wasn't back at my desk in the office for more than three minutes when the phone jangled. It was a *Post* reporter who reminded me that we had met a few years back at a cocktail party in Lily Rowan's duplex. I didn't remember him.

"Hey, Archie, how about putting your boss on the line? I know he doesn't go upstairs to play with his orchids until four. See . . . I've done my homework. The city editor is on my case to get some quotes about the Cameron Clay death. You know how it is."

"No, I really don't know how it is, never having had the privilege of working on a newspaper. I guess I will have to live with that void in my life. And sorry to report, but Mr. Wolfe is not available."

"Aw, come on, be a pal and give me a break. By the way, how's your gal Lily these days?"

That did it. I quietly cradled my instrument, turning to Wolfe. "The beat goes on," I said. "How does it feel to be the most popular man in New York City and its environs with the disseminators of news and sometimes scandal?"

Apparently, my question was not enough to tear him away from his current book, *All Creatures Great and Small*, by James Herriot. "Look, I know you're engrossed in what must be a captivating volume, but you said we would talk after lunch. It is now after lunch. I thought it might be fun if I went to work."

The doorbell rang again, but this time it was relatively good news: A bicycle messenger delivering Clay's key in an envelope. I thanked him and tipped him, then called Saul.

"Are you up to rifling a home this afternoon?"

"Let me take a wild guess: The residence in question belonged to the late Cameron Clay."

"You're a winner, as usual. Can you meet me there in an hour?" I gave him the address.

"See you then," Saul said.

I took a cab to Chelsea and climbed out just as Saul was walking up. "You should be getting more exercise, Archie," he told me. "There is nothing like taking a brisk stroll on a February day to invigorate a person."

"I'll have to take your word for that. Let us see what awaits us within."

Clay's brownstone was probably half the size of Wolfe's, and not nearly as nice, which we were to learn. We started on the first floor, noting the living-room sofa where the columnist's body had been found. The two end-table drawers were empty except for some matchbooks, and the bookshelf had only a half dozen volumes, mostly detective and spy novels. We went through each book, but nothing fell out, no suicide note or an angry letter threatening bodily harm.

The kitchen looked like it was rarely used, except for a toaster on a counter surrounded by crumbs, a coffeepot that looked like it hadn't been scrubbed out since the Boer War, and one bottle each of gin, rye, and dry vermouth, all of which were about half full. The refrigerator contained bread, butter, a can of coffee, and a bottle of orange juice, nothing more. The sink was full of dirty plates, cups, glasses, and silverware.

The rest of the three-story abode was similarly devoid of interest. In fact, much of the place did not seem lived in at all, raising the question of why its owner needed so much space. Two of the three upstairs bedrooms had no sign whatever of being used, and Clay's room was Spartan, its closet holding only three sport coats, several pairs of slacks, a half dozen shirts, and three pairs of shoes. The chest of drawers held nothing more interesting than underwear, socks, and handkerchiefs. The top of the chest was a repository for keys, coins, a tarnished money clip containing forty-seven dollars, three packs of cigarettes—one of them opened—an ashtray filled with butts, and a Metropolitan Trust Company checkbook showing a balance of slightly more than eleven hundred dollars.

The other room on the top floor was an office of sorts, with peeling wallpaper, a battered oak desk on which sat an ancient Underwood typewriter, a pile of copy paper, and a small stack of letters from readers, all of them complimentary. Presumably, Clay planned to answer them, or perhaps he already had.

Saul and I turned every mattress. We also went through every drawer in the house, checking to see if any of them had false bottoms—none did. "Anything we've missed?" I asked Saul after we had been there for three-quarters of an hour.

"I can't imagine what. It's what I didn't see that struck me."

"Such as?"

"The guy did nothing whatever to personalize the place. There is no art on the walls and not a single photograph anywhere."

"Knowing what I do about Clay, I hardly expected a 'Home Sweet Home' sampler hanging on one wall," I said.

"True, we already knew that the man was something of a loner, but somehow I expected to learn more about him."

"Well, the kitchen tells us he was a slob who liked martinis and rye, his bedroom tells us he was no Beau Brummel, and the overall emptiness of the place says he didn't spend much time here, except to sleep and grab a quick and very light breakfast. He probably spent at least ten hours a day in his office at the *Gazette* or attending some evening function or another in search of items for his column."

"Seems like a pretty sad life," Saul observed.

"I agree. But then, not everybody is like you. Your stately dwelling place only a few blocks from here is a true bachelor's nirvana: grand piano; ceiling-high bookcases filled with honest-to-goodness books you have read, many of them classics; an eight-sided, felt-topped poker table; a stereo system; Impressionist and Cubist paintings on the walls; a well-stocked bar; and a wine cellar that's superior to those at some of this town's fine restaurants."

Saul tried to look embarrassed, but it didn't work. "Okay, so I like a few nice things. You got a problem with that?"

"Yes I do, it's called the sin of envy."

CHAPTER 15

When Wolfe came down from the plant rooms at six, I told him of our fruitless visit to Cameron Clay's home. He did not seem surprised.

"All right," Wolf said with a sigh. "It is time to tackle the five people we discussed earlier. The first one I desire to talk to is Mr. Michael Tobin."

"I assume you prefer a face-to-face conversation, rather than a telephone chat, correct?"

Wolfe had turned back to his book, so I took his answer to be "yes."

I was not about to call the disgraced former cop, and although I had his address in Yonkers, I wanted more, which meant another call to Lon.

"You're going to be hearing a lot from me in the days ahead," I told him.

"I will try to hide my surprise," he said. "What is it this time?"

"I want the address of that florist shop in Yonkers where Tobin has been working. I plan to pay him a visit."

Lon cursed but quickly apologized. "Sorry, Archie, I realize that you're working on behalf of my bosses. I'll have to call you back." He did, less than five minutes later, with what I needed.

"If you're interested, I'm off to Yonkers," I told Wolfe. I can only assume he heard me because he didn't look up from the book.

I made the short hike over to Curran's Motors on Tenth Avenue between Thirty-Fifth and Thirty-Sixth Streets, where Wolfe has garaged his cars for years, and I got the Heron sedan. Ten minutes later, I was headed north on the West Side Highway, which then became the Henry Hudson Parkway and finally the Saw Mill River Parkway by the time it entered Yonkers.

I had no trouble finding Broadway in this suburban city. The florist shop was wedged between a hardware store and a dry cleaner on a busy commercial stretch. I parked a block away and walked to the store, which displayed several colorful floral arrangements in its front window. Peering in, I saw a lone figure behind the counter, waiting on a woman. I had seen enough photographs of Michael Tobin in the newspapers to recognize his square, ruddy face and permanently pugnacious expression. Stepping into the store, I played the browser while Tobin and the customer transacted their business. After she thanked him and left with her purchase, I walked to the counter. "You are Michael Tobin," I said.

"Yes . . ." He was guarded as he eyed me under thick eyebrows.

"My name is Archie Goodwin, and I work for the detective Nero Wolfe. Perhaps you've heard of him."

"What is it you want?" he said through clenched teeth as he tensed up.

"Mr. Wolfe is investigating the death of Cameron Clay, the *Gazette* columnist."

"I know who he is—or was," Tobin snarled. "What's to investigate? The man killed himself."

"Maybe. Anyway, it seems that the late Mr. Clay had been getting anonymous telephone calls threatening his life, and he had named five individuals as candidates for making those calls. You are one of the five."

"Listen, you cheap gumshoe, don't try to get tough with me."

"I wouldn't think of it, Mr. Tobin. I am simply a messenger, nothing more. Mr. Wolfe would like to talk to you."

"Is that so? Well tell your fat boss not to bother calling me, because I won't answer."

"He doesn't want to call you; he wants to see you, in his office."

I thought Tobin was going to have a coronary attack. "Are you out of your goddamn mind? Go tell him that he can stuff it."

"Well, I certainly had not expected this reaction, Mr. Tobin. You see: all four of the others on Mr. Clay's list have been to see Nero Wolfe. They had no problem talking to him. If it were to get into the newspapers that you were the only one who—"

"And you're telling me it *would* get into the newspapers," Tobin rasped, beads of sweat breaking out on his freckled forehead.

"Given your, well . . . past history, I shouldn't think you would want any further publicity in the press. And as you may know, Mr. Wolfe is very well connected with newspaper executives in New York."

I really hadn't expected the guy to crumble, but apparently I had him on the ropes, so I moved in for the knockout. "You are not being accused of anything, but Mr. Wolfe feels it's important that he speak to people who may have for one reason or another held a grudge against Cameron Clay. It is possible you will have some helpful information for him."

"I don't have any information of any kind!" he yelled.

"All right, Mr. Tobin, if that's the way you want it. Your name will almost surely appear in at least one New York paper tomorrow as one who refuses to cooperate with an investigation."

"Hah! It's not a police investigation, it is a damned private eye drumming up business."

"Do you honestly think readers will differentiate between types of inquiries? And do you really want your name involved, even in an indirect way, with the death of someone you had been quoted as disliking intensely?"

"So you'd dredge up the past to make me seem guilty of something in the present, is that how you play?"

"Nobody has said anything about your being guilty, but if you fail to sit down with Nero Wolfe and word gets out, how do you think that will look?"

"And, of course, you're suggesting that word will get out, right?" Tobin growled, his large white-knuckled hands gripping the counter.

"I am suggesting only that it would be a very good idea for you to have a conversation with Nero Wolfe."

"And just where would this conversation be held?"

"In the office of Mr. Wolfe's brownstone on West Thirty-Fifth Street." I gave him the address.

"Oh, swell! In an office that's bugged, of course!"

"No, sir. Nero Wolfe has not ever bugged a meeting in his office, and he never will."

"And I suppose I'm supposed to take your word for that?" Tobin sneered.

"If you don't believe me, ask Inspector Cramer about Wolfe's credibility."

"That'll never happen," he laughed sourly. "I doubt if Cramer would give me the time of day, let alone information about a private cop."

"All I can say to you is that you can trust Mr. Wolfe to keep your session with him confidential."

Tobin looked down at the linoleum countertop for several seconds and then back up at me. "When would this meeting take place?"

"Tonight, nine o'clock."

"Who would be present?"

"You, me, and Nero Wolfe. No one else."

He took a deep breath, then another. More seconds went by. "All right, give me the damned address. I'll be there. But by God, if I don't like the way things are going, I'm out of there, fast."

"Fair enough. We will see you at nine."

As I drove home, I counted the number of lies and misrepresentations I had thrown Tobin's way and hoped they would not come back to haunt me on the judgment day.

CHAPTER 16

When I got back to the brownstone, Wolfe was up in the plant rooms. "Anybody call in my absence?" I asked Fritz in the kitchen.

"Yes, a very rude man from a radio station, and a woman, also very demanding and unpleasant, from some newspaper over in New Jersey that I have never heard of. They both insisted on speaking to Mr. Wolfe."

"And you told them to shove it."

"No, Archie, I refuse to answer bad manners with more bad manners. But I was firm with them."

"You are a better man, and a nicer man, than I am, Gunga Din."

"Ah, a play on the writings of Mr. Rudyard Kipling, Archie. Do you like his work?"

Fritz's knowledge in all sorts of areas continues to amaze me. In answer to his question, I sheepishly replied, "I've never read him."

Wolfe came down from the plant rooms at six and, of course, immediately rang for beer.

"We will be having a visitor later," I said nonchalantly as he settled into his chair.

"Indeed?"

"Former New York City Police Captain 'Iron Mike' Tobin."

Wolfe raised his eyebrows. "Satisfactory."

For those of you unfamiliar with Nero Wolfe's mannerisms, his mouthing of "satisfactory" is equivalent to a normal person saying "marvelous" or "hearty congratulations." And on those rare occasions when he says "very satisfactory," it equates to "hallelujah."

"How did you persuade Mr. Tobin to grace us with his presence?" Wolfe asked.

"More than once, you have advised me—make that *told* me—to use my intelligence, guided by my experience. That is what I did. The result is that he will be here at nine, or so he said. He was less than ecstatic with the idea of coming to see you, though."

"Hardly surprising," Wolfe observed. "Mr. Tobin is by no means a paragon. However, he will be treated in the same fashion as any guest under this roof."

Wolfe may often be irascible—a word Inspector Cramer has used more than once to describe him—but he is steadfast in his insistence that in his home "a guest is a jewel, resting on the cushion of hospitality." Some jewel, this disgraced former cop. But then, this is Nero Wolfe's house, and he makes the rules. If I ever own my own place, which is highly unlikely at this stage, I will make my own rules, and not every guest will be a jewel resting on a cushion of any kind.

That night, as the clock crawled toward nine, I was giving myself no better than even odds that Tobin would show up.

Sure, I thought I had done a pretty good sales job on him, but then, he had time to think about it and maybe decided he would take his chances and stay away.

I would be lying if I told you I didn't breathe a sigh of relief when the doorbell rang at two minutes to nine. I went down the hall and saw a glowering Michael Tobin, late of the New York City Police Department, through the one-way glass. "Come in," I said, trying to force a smile. "You are right on time."

"Yeah, well I do happen to know my way around this town," Tobin muttered, not bothering to fake a smile. He stomped in, saw the rack, and hung his coat and hat on it. "Okay, dammit, let's get on with this crap. Where's your boss?"

"Follow me." I led him to the office and motioned toward the red leather chair, which he dropped into.

"Is he going to keep me waiting?" Tobin demanded.

"I am not, Mr. Tobin," Wolfe said as he walked in and moved around behind his desk, sitting. "I am about to have beer. Would you like something to drink?"

"Trying to get me drunk, are you?"

"Not at all, sir. I assume you are a man of the world, fully capable of holding your alcohol. But if you prefer to abstain, that is your prerogative."

That drew a guttural laugh. "Ah, hell, sure I'll have something," Tobin said, turning to me. "You know how to make a martini?"

"I've been mixing them for people for years," I told him as Wolfe made a face. He thinks anyone who drinks gin is a barbarian—and that includes me when I have the occasional gin and tonic on a summer day. I made Tobin's martini and handed it to him, getting a slight nod of thanks.

Fritz came in with Wolfe's beer, and after he opened one of the two bottles and poured it into a glass, he considered Tobin. "Mr. Goodwin explained why I wanted to see you?"

"In a fashion," he gruffed. "It seems you think that cheap columnist was murdered, and the fact that I'm here means that you believe that I'm a suspect."

"You did not like Mr. Clay."

"Hah, now there's an understatement if I ever heard one! The man was a bastard, plain and simple."

"When you were in prison, you were heard to say that you would 'get' Cameron Clay if it was the last thing you did."

"A lot is said when you're inside," Tobin answered with the wave of a hand. "I can tell you this, though: If it hadn't been for that S.O.B., I never would have served time, not a minute of it. The case against me was weak, but Clay's constant shots at me influenced the jury, I'm positive of that. It was a case of trial by newspaper."

"You deny brutalizing prisoners?"

"Hell, I may have roughed a few of them up all right, I won't deny it, and so did plenty of others on the force. But if you knew what some of those lowlifes had done to their victims, you'd have roughed them up, too."

"Can you account for your time when Mr. Clay died?" Wolfe asked.

"That was . . . when?"

"Last Tuesday night and the early hours of Wednesday."

"Uh, yeah, I was home watching television until about midnight and then I went to bed."

"Was someone with you?"

"No, I was the only one home. My wife was visiting her sister in Ohio for about a week. So there I am, without an alibi. Why don't you call Cramer and have the inspector himself come over to put the cuffs on me? He's never liked me anyway."

"The official position of the police department, and that includes Inspector Cramer, is that Mr. Clay killed himself."

"But obviously, someone else thinks otherwise, or you wouldn't be talking to me. By the way, how many people know I'm here?" Tobin demanded, leaning forward and slapping a palm down on the desktop.

"Only Mr. Goodwin and me."

"Yeah? I know from Goodwin that you've talked to other suspects. What did they tell you?"

"Really, Mr. Tobin. Do you expect an answer to that question? I would no more reveal what other people have said in this office than I would tell anyone else the content of my conversation with you."

"Okay, then tell me this: How many people do you think could have bumped off Clay?"

"I will not respond to that question, either."

Another harsh laugh. "Maybe that's because there are probably dozens in this town who would have liked to get rid of him, maybe even more. Did you ever meet the bastard?"

"Yes, once."

"Once should have been enough for you to see what a miserable, detestable skunk he was."

"You certainly sound like someone who disliked Cameron Clay enough to murder him," Wolfe said.

"I did not kill him, Wolfe, but make no mistake—I am not sorry for a second that he's dead," Tobin said. "If that makes me a suspect in your eyes, I can't help it."

"I appreciate your candor, sir, although I must say that without an alibi for several critical hours, you may indeed find yourself taking on the role of a suspect at some point."

Tobin took a drink and snorted. "Once convicted, forever presumed guilty of anything else, right? Hell, we moved out of New York City proper because of the way our neighbors looked at us and shunned my wife. But it's not much better up in sweet old Yonkers. Oh sure, I've got a buddy who gave me some work in that flower shop, but we still get looks from neighbors. If it wasn't for her loyal bridge club ladies, my wife wouldn't have any friends. I sure don't have many anymore myself."

"According to an item in one of Mr. Clay's columns, you seem to have a friend in Aldo Marshall, or should we refer to him as Aldo Moretti?" Wolfe said.

Tobin went rigid. "Yeah, I know all about that."

"Was the item about you taking a trip to the Caribbean with Mr. Marshall correct?"

"It was. We're old friends."

"So I gather. Should one raise questions about a former police officer being an old friend of a major figure in the crime syndicate?" Wolfe asked.

"I got nothing to say about that."

"I've heard and read that a lot of cops feel you got a raw deal," I said, "so there are still people on your side. A number of them wrote letters in the papers defending you and criticizing Clay."

"Yeah, that was nice to know, even if it didn't do me one damned bit of good. Say, Goodwin, you make a hell of a martini," Tobin said, holding up his glass in salute.

"Want another?"

"Sure, why not," he said, turning to Wolfe. "You got any more questions to throw at me?"

"For purposes of discussion, let us assume you had nothing to do with Mr. Clay's death. Would you care to speculate on anyone else's involvement?"

Tobin shrugged. "I wouldn't know where to start, other than maybe that black councilman from Harlem—what's his name, Beardsley. He got ripped in Clay's *Gazette* column about as often as I did. Beyond him, there's at least twenty others who he's torn into from time to time. One thing I'm curious about," he continued, pausing to sip his second martini. "What makes you so sure this was murder? My old employers seem convinced it was a suicide, at least based on what I've been reading, which is my only source these days. It will hardly surprise you to learn that I have no pipelines into the department any more. In fact, if the brass at 240 Centre Street never hear my name again, it will be too soon."

"In answer to your question, I am not convinced Mr. Clay was murdered, but there is reason to doubt that he did away with himself."

"I suppose it's fruitless to ask, but I will anyway: Who is your client?"

"You are correct, sir, in that asking will bear you no fruit."

CHAPTER 17

Well, what do you think of him?" I asked Wolfe as I returned to the office after walking Tobin down the hall and locking the front door behind him.

"He was basically as I expected, somewhat surly, unrepentant, defensive, and probably one who did not get along well with most of his superior officers."

"For starters, we already know that Cramer didn't much care for him, to say the least."

"We have had our differences with the inspector over the years, but you know as well as I do that he is honest and, I believe, unimpeachable. He is fervent in upholding the integrity of the police department and would naturally detest anyone who brought shame upon it, as Mr. Tobin so manifestly did."

"You really nailed him on that trip to the Caribbean with the mobster Marshall. He didn't even try to deny it. Also, he seems to feel that the only reason he was convicted was because of Clay's columns and their influence on the jury."

"He envisions himself as a victim rather than as a perpetrator, as is so often the case with miscreants," Wolfe said. "Man's ability to indulge in self-deception knows no bounds."

"Nice. Who said that?"

"I did, unless, of course, I was subconsciously parroting the words of one of the Greek philosophers, which I concede is possible although unlikely."

"Whatever you do, don't go out on a limb. All right, so for now we place Michael Tobin, late of the New York City Police Department, on our 'maybe' list of suspects. Who would you like me to haul in next?"

Wolfe leaned back, shutting his eyes. For just a moment, I thought he was going to begin that exercise where he pushes his lips in and out, in and out, and then after a period ranging from twelve minutes to just more than an hour—I know, I've timed every one of these exercises over the years—he opens his eyes and has solved the mystery. Not so this time, however. There was to be no denouement tonight.

"That councilman, Millard Beardsley, I want to see him next," Wolfe said, blinking. "Tomorrow, if possible."

"Would you like to see him in the morning, the afternoon, or the evening?" I asked in what I hoped was a bland tone.

"The evening is, of course, preferable," he said. "Nine o'clock would be the optimum time."

I briefly contemplated picking up my typewriter and throwing it at him, but figured that if I missed and it got dented, he would deduct the cost of a new one from my paycheck, so I settled on making a face at him, which he did not see because his book was in the way.

■ ■ ■

After breakfast the next morning, I called the phone number I was given by Lon for Councilman Millard Beardsley. "Mr. Beardsley's District Office, may I help you?" came a soft, sweet voice that was pleasant on the ears.

"Would I by chance be able to speak to Mr. Beardsley in person today?" I asked her.

"You certainly would, sir," she said in her soft-as-suede tone. "This just happens to be one of Mr. Beardsley's twice-monthly 'I'm Here to Meet My Public' days in our district office on 125th Street, starting at ten o'clock. Your timing is very good, sir; that is, if you are able to come here today."

I could have listened to her voice for an hour, but I decided to forgo the pleasure and got the address from her. Twenty minutes later, I was in a northbound yellow cab, destination Harlem. Beardsley's office was a storefront just a block down the busy main commercial street of Harlem from the famous theater and its marquee topped by the red letters vertically spelling out APOLLO.

Peering through the windows, I saw that perhaps a dozen people stood inside, apparently in a line. I entered and was met immediately by a smiling black man in a double-breasted suit and tie. "Good morning, sir, are you here to see the councilman?" he said.

"I am, if that is not a problem." I had noted without surprise that everyone ahead of me in the line that led to Millard Beardsley was black.

"It is not a problem, not at all, sir. Mr. Beardsley makes time for everyone who comes to see him. Please be patient. He often spends many minutes speaking with a constituent about some problem. Are you by any chance a constituent of Mr. Beardsley's?"

"No, I am not, but I am a resident and a registered voter in this city, have been for many years, and I have a problem that I would like to discuss with him."

"The councilman often spends time here with people outside his district. I am sure that he will be happy to talk to you."

As I moved slowly ahead in the line that led ultimately to Millard Beardsley, I noticed a fetching young woman with a chocolate complexion talking on the telephone at a desk off on one side in the unadorned room. I couldn't hear everything she was saying because of the chattering that went on among those ahead of me in line, but I did hear enough to know she was the sweet-voiced person who had answered when I called. I nodded toward her, but she was engrossed in her conversation and did not look in my direction.

I was now the second person in line, which gave me the opportunity to study the councilman. He sat on a folding chair behind a mahogany table, while a burly, thick-necked man, the only other white person in the room, stood behind and slightly to one side of him, arms folded across his barrel chest. Obviously a bodyguard.

The table at which Beardsley sat had two other folding chairs in front of it, one of which currently was occupied by a heavy-set woman of middle age whose complaints about her landlord were punctuated by sobs and the occasional "I swear that man is Satan himself!"

Beardsley, balding and mustachioed and with elbows resting on the table, cupped his hands on his chin and listened to the woman's grievances as if she were the only person in the world at that moment. He nodded and occasionally inserted a comforting word. Finally, she ran down like an alarm clock, and he took one of her hands between his, squeezing it.

"You have a most valid reason for your distress, Mrs. Robinson, and I assure you that I am going to personally look into this. Will you kindly give us your address and telephone number—do you have a telephone?" She nodded. "Give your address and telephone number to April over there, and then I will know how to reach you, which I most assuredly will do." He indicated the lovely young woman who still was on the telephone.

"God bless you, Mr. Beardsley," she said, standing and sniffling. "I just knew that when you heard my story, you would help me. God bless all of your family, too." The councilman stood and took her hand between his again, kissing it and assuring her that he would do everything he could to see that she got justice. Then he turned to me with raised eyebrows, undoubtedly puzzled as to why a man with my complexion would be at his "I'm Here to Meet My Public" event.

"My name is Archie Goodwin," I said. "I work for the private detective Nero Wolfe. He wants to talk to you about the death of Cameron Clay."

"I have heard of Mr. Wolfe, of course, but why in the world would he want to speak to me about that . . . newspaper columnist, Mr. Goodwin?" Beardsley asked, rising. "I did not know the man, and what little I have read about his death points to it being a suicide."

"I only know that Mr. Wolfe feels you might be able to provide some information regarding Mr. Clay's demise."

"I could choose to be insulted by that suggestion, sir. I see no reason whatever to discuss anything with Nero Wolfe, although I bear him no animosity whatever."

"Cameron Clay had been receiving threatening telephone calls in the weeks before his death, and he suspected they could have been from any one of five individuals. You were one of those he suspected."

"That's it!" the bodyguard barked, coming forward and giving me a shove in the chest with a hand the size of a skillet.

"You've been bothering Mr. Beardsley long enough." He took a swing at me, but I dodged it. The man was fullback-size, but also fullback-slow. I slipped under the punch, grabbed one of his arms, and spun him around, getting the arm in a hammerlock. He yelped as I put pressure on, and his knees began to buckle.

"Stop it, both of you!" Beardsley yelled. "I will not have violence in here. There is enough violence on the streets and in the homes all around us. Now, you two, shake hands."

The bodyguard glared at me but didn't put out a paw. "Charles, shake hands with Mr. Goodwin—now!"

I didn't want to bury the hatchet any more than Charles did, but we shook hands, our faces grim, and damned if the others who had been in line behind me actually broke into applause.

"That is better, much better," Beardsley said approvingly. "Now Mr. Goodwin, sit down. Let us talk for a few minutes, but only for a few. There are others here who I need to be seeing." He nodded toward those who were in line behind me.

In a voice just above a whisper, given the proximity of those in the queue, I told Beardsley that Wolfe already had held discussions with the other four who Clay had been suspicious of.

"As I said earlier, I have heard of Nero Wolfe before, and I've read about him in the papers over the years, too. Who hasn't? From what I know, he rarely leaves his home."

"That is correct."

"So if I were to see him, it would be where he lives, is that it?"

"Yes, sir. I can give you the address."

Beardsley bit his lower lip as if weighing his options, then he sighed. "All right, Mr. Goodwin. I will come to see the great Nero Wolfe. When are you suggesting we meet?"

"He would really like to see you tonight. Say nine o'clock."

"You do not believe in dragging things out, do you?"

"Mr. Wolfe doesn't. I am only his messenger."

"Very well. I will call upon him tonight, but I will not be bullied. Is that understood, Mr. Goodwin?"

"No one can be bullied who doesn't want to be," I said.

That brought a tight smile from the councilman, who turned to his sulking bodyguard. "Charles, please go out and hail a taxi for Mr. Goodwin. He is our guest.

"Now, who is next?" he said, looking at the line. "Ah, Mr. Phillips, so good to see you again. Please sit down and tell me if you were able to settle your insurance claim. I called the company and was very stern with the gentleman I spoke to. I do hope it brought the desired results. I will not have my constituents pushed around by big, impersonal institutions."

CHAPTER 18

Charles flagged a taxi for me as ordered, but he was not happy about it. Not a word got exchanged between us before I climbed into a yellow cab and gave the hackie the brownstone's address.

By the time I got back home, Wolfe had come down from his morning session with his "concubines," as he refers to those ten thousand orchids thriving three flights above us. He was at his desk with beer and the *London Times* crossword puzzle when I eased into my chair and told him Councilman Millard Beardsley would be calling on us that night. I half expected another "satisfactory," but the realist in me knew that he doles out those accolades sparingly, lest they lose their impact.

Instead, he asked for my impressions of the councilman. "I know, of course, that Cameron Clay had no use for him, but I was impressed with what little I saw of his interaction with his constituents. He seems to have an extremely loyal following in

Harlem and the surrounding areas. And he has been reelected several times."

"So have numerous other public servants who do not necessarily merit their long tenures," Wolfe observed.

"You mean it's often the case of the devil you know as opposed to the devil you don't know?"

"I would not have phrased it in that manner, but the observation will suffice. Once an individual has been elected to office, it becomes very difficult to dislodge him."

"There's plenty of them who ought to be dislodged," I said. "I'm not sure whether Millard Beardsley is one of those, but I will be interested in your reaction to him."

Millard Beardsley rang our doorbell that night at three minutes to nine. I was relieved when I looked through the one-way glass to see that he was alone, although a Lincoln idled at the curb. I had been afraid he might have decided to bring Charles or another bodyguard. One hammerlock a day was plenty, although it had been harder on Charles than on me.

"Good evening, Mr. Beardsley," I said, opening the door to him. "Please come in."

The councilman seemed neither angry nor pleased. He nodded curtly, doffed his hat, and shucked off his overcoat. I hung up his things and directed him down the hall to the office, where he took the red leather chair without asking.

"Mr. Wolfe will be in shortly. He is just finishing up some other business," I said.

"No, he isn't," Beardsley said without apparent resentment as he crossed one leg over the other. "He just wants to make a grand entrance. I do the same thing myself all the time. There is no shame in that, nor do I resent it in someone else."

As if on cue, Wolfe walked in. "Good evening, sir," he said

as he detoured around the desk to his chair. "Would you like something to drink? I am having beer."

"The best scotch that you have got," Beardsley replied coolly, "and straight up, please. Adding water to good liquor is a sin."

"Archie," Wolfe said without a pause, "you heard the gentleman."

I drink scotch, but I'm no expert about it. However, I do know how much dedicated scotch drinkers swear allegiance to single malts, so that is what I chose from the serving cart and poured for our guest.

"Wonderful," Beardsley said after taking a sip. He pronounced the brand, although he had not seen the bottle, and I confirmed it to him.

"Mr. Goodwin has told you of the purpose of this meeting, I believe," Wolfe said.

"He did. You apparently believe I had something to do with the death of Cameron Clay."

"Did Mr. Goodwin say that?"

"Not in so many words."

"I thought not. This is no inquisition, sir, although I believe it is fair to say that you did not like Mr. Clay."

Beardsley took a second sip of his scotch and set the glass down carefully. "I never met Cameron Clay, although he certainly chose to consistently excoriate me in his columns."

"You have been called the city's best-known and hardest-working councilman," Wolfe said, "although not by Mr. Clay."

"True, that was said of me in a local magazine sometime back."

"So you have received some praise. Mr. Clay, however, criticized your poor attendance record in the City Council, among other things."

"If you had ever attended a council meeting, you would

know why I so often choose to stay away. Almost nothing gets done in those sessions; they are a waste of time. I can serve my constituents much better by staying in the district and working for them. Your Mr. Goodwin here saw me in action this morning, having one-on-one meetings with people who need practical help. And I can give them help—and hope."

"A most handsome speech, sir. But your poor record of attendance at City Council meetings was not the only area in which Mr. Clay found fault with you."

Beardsley tilted his head to one side as if digesting Wolfe's comment; no doubt a practiced gesture. "Mr. Clay had a great deal to say about me in print, most of it innuendo and downright lies. It is very easy for someone with the kind of following he had to write anything he feels like, and people will believe it, particularly if they are racists. And there are a lot of racists around."

"Did you ever sue him?" Wolfe asked.

"What good would it have done?" Beardsley said, turning a palm up. "If there were a trial, it would have turned into a circus, and even were I to win, and I'm sure I would have, it would distract me for days, maybe even weeks, from working on behalf of the people in my district. As you must know, those I serve are among the neediest in the city."

"Do you have close ties with those in what is often referred to as the underworld?"

Beardsley laughed. "Ah yes, yet another of Mr. Cameron Clay's frequent allegations. In my position, I have come to know people in all walks, and it is indeed possible that some of them may have had 'ties,' as you term it, with criminal elements. Bear in mind that I have for years worked with convicted felons to help them reenter society after their prison terms, and so, of course, I've come to know many people who have lived much of their lives outside the law."

"A facile response," Wolfe said. "Have any of those who have 'lived outside the law,' to use your phrase, ever approached you offering to deal with Cameron Clay on your behalf?"

Another laugh from the councilman, this one louder than the first. "You just won't let loose of this bone, will you? What puzzles me is why you are so damned intent on proving that Clay was murdered when the police seem to be convinced that it was suicide."

"I have a client who does not happen to agree with the police," Wolfe said.

"Yes? And who might that client be?"

"Come, come, Mr. Beardsley. I would no more divulge that to you than I would tell anyone you had been a visitor here."

"Code of honor, huh? Well, all I can tell you is that I had nothing whatever to do with Cameron Clay's death. Am I sorry that he's gone? Not in the least. I would be a liar if I stated otherwise."

"I appreciate your candor, sir."

"And why not be candid? I am on record as saying that Clay was an enemy of the black community. He denied it, of course, but I believe his columns have spoken volumes about his true feelings. Like so many other white men, he resented any black man who had attained a measure of success, as I have. If that sounds arrogant of me, I plead guilty. I do not believe in false modesty."

"Nor do I," Wolfe said. "For purposes of discussion, let us stipulate that Mr. Clay was murdered. Can you suggest a possible candidate as the killer?"

Yet another laugh, one I would term a guffaw. "Now it is my turn to say 'come, come,' Mr. Wolfe. Where to start? Cameron Clay had alienated so many people in so many different areas that I wouldn't even begin to speculate. And if I did, I certainly would not want to be quoted."

"I would not quote you, sir, but I agree that the columnist made a great many enemies, and he appears to have relished doing so."

"I am sure that he relished it. At the risk of sounding rude, and I do not mean to do so, I don't believe I can be of any further use to you in this endeavor."

"Thank you for coming, Mr. Beardsley," Wolfe said as the councilman rose, smiled tightly, and left the office with me close behind him.

"Well, what are your impressions of New York's best-known and hardest-working councilman?" I posed to Wolfe after seeing Beardsley out.

"He is one secure in his legacy as a defender of the underdog and the downtrodden. Also, for all of his apparent candor, I would not trust his word on anything of more import than a weather forecast, and even on that, I would also check with another source."

"Yeah, I concur. On the surface, he seems as earnest as a small-town family doctor, but scratch that surface and you have a used-car salesman or a television-ad pitchman. Well, what's next?"

"Three people remain on our list. I leave it to you to pursue them in any order, and the sooner the better. But first, talk to the cab driver Mr. Clay used as his personal chauffeur. Find out if he has any insights as to the columnist's moods in his last days."

"Your wish is my command," I told him, getting up and going to the kitchen for a glass of milk before turning in.

CHAPTER 19

In the morning after breakfast, I dialed the number Larry McNeil had given me for Clay's cabbie, Walter Bartlett. I figured he'd be out on the street at this hour, but to my surprise, he answered the phone.

"Yeah, I'm Bartlett," he said in a sleepy voice. "What d'ya want?"

I explained who I was and why I wanted to see him, then asked if we could meet somewhere. "Geez, I . . . I guess so, although I don't know that I can be much help to you. But if somebody killed Mr. Clay, I'd like to see the bastard fry for it." Bartlett lived over in Queens, but he was going to work the noon to midnight shift today and would take the subway to West Seventy-Eighth Street to pick up his hack at the yellow-cab garage there. He suggested we meet at a coffee shop just east of the garage. "I'll be the guy in a brown flat cap sitting in a booth by the window," he said.

When I walked into the café forty-five minutes later, a little, hunched-over guy with a mustache and a flat cap held up a hand. "I figured right off that it was you," Bartlett said as I slid into the booth opposite him. "This place gets almost all regulars, majority of 'em cabbies, and we don't see too many suit-and-tie types in here. Not that that ain't okay," he added quickly.

We each ordered coffee, and I went to work. "You must have gotten to know Cameron Clay quite well, driving him to and from the office every day."

"Well, at least *to* the office," Bartlett said. "Some nights he went to parties and stuff like that, so I didn't always take him home."

"How did he seem, in the days leading up to . . . what happened? Did you see a change in him?"

The cabbie shrugged. "I guess. Seems like he'd gotten quieter. When I first started driving him two, three years ago, he was pretty chatty, used to even ask my opinion on things going on around town." Bartlett laughed. "Sometimes, he even put something in his column about me, like 'My hack driver, Walter, thinks New York motorists are ruder than ever.' Stuff like that. Made me feel like a celebrity."

"Did Clay ever talk about people who didn't like him?"

"Yeah, once in a while. He'd say things like, 'Walter, I know damned well there's lots of folks out there who'd like nothing more than to push me off a cliff or stick a knife in me. Well, screw 'em all.'"

"He never mentioned anyone in particular?"

"I can't recall it, no."

"What about his health?"

Bartlett ran a hand over the stubble on his cheek. "You

could tell he wasn't in good shape. In the last few weeks, he seemed to be wheezing more, and coughing quite a bit."

"As you know if you read the papers, the police think Cameron Clay killed himself."

"So I been reading. I don't believe it. No, sir, I don't. I figure one of those people who didn't like him did the job."

"Did you drive him home the night he died?"

"Yes, I did. He actually seemed okay, very relaxed and a little peppier than he had been lately. He was in a good mood and laughed about how bad the Knicks had been playing lately. 'They need a whole new team,' he said."

I thanked Bartlett for his time and paid the check. The cabbie and I walked out together, and he put a hand on my arm. "You should know, Mr. Goodwin, that Mr. Clay was very good to me. Gave me big tips and a Christmas bonus, and when my wife was sick, he gave me extra—a lot extra—to help cover the hospital bills. He was a fine man."

By the time I got back to the brownstone, Wolfe was down from the plant room and in the process of opening his first beer of the day. I filled him in on my conversation with Walter Bartlett and he responded by saying nothing other than to remind me I had three more "enemies" of Cameron Clay to entice to the brownstone.

I looked at those remaining names and decided, for no particular reason, to tackle the lawyer, Roswell Stokes, next. For help with this, I turned to our own longtime attorney, Nathaniel Parker.

"You and your boss in some kind of trouble again?" Parker said when I reached him in his office. "Seems like that's the only time I ever hear from you."

"Not true," I said, pointing out that he had dined with us a few months back and had raved at length about the Cape Cod clam cakes.

"Point taken, Archie. That was a meal to remember, as Fritz's so often are," Parker said. "I withdraw my earlier comment and hereby beg the court's forgiveness. What can I do for you?"

"For reasons I cannot go into at present, I need to talk, preferably in person, to one Roswell Stokes."

"Ah, so you would have dealings with the Vulture? At some point down the road, I'd be most interested in learning what that is all about."

"The Vulture, eh?"

"That is what he's known as in our legal circles. He goes after big fees with the same ruthless, single-minded determination with which vultures devour their prey. Unfortunately for you, I don't know Stokes well enough—nor do I care to—to set up a meeting."

"That's not what I'm shooting for. I assume he eats lunch out."

"I suppose so."

"I would like to learn where he eats, and then approach him in a restaurant."

"I may actually be of some help there. An old law school classmate of mine is a partner in his firm, Mason, Chalmers, and Stokes. I can find out from him if Stokes does dine out, and if so, where. Did you have a specific date in mind?"

"Yes, today, if possible."

"Well, make no small plans! All right, Archie, I'll take advantage of the good old college connection and see what I can come up with."

Parker called me back fifteen minutes later. "Roswell Stokes has a one o'clock reservation at the Melrose Club on East Fifty-

Fourth Street. He eats there almost every day, according to my source."

"Damn, a private club! That's what I was afraid of."

"No, no, it's not, although it tends to act like one. It is very clubby in appearance, a lot of dark paneling and bookcases and subdued lighting, but it's a restaurant open to the public. I've eaten there numerous times, and the food is absolutely first-rate. Wait . . . let me amend that. It is first-rate to most people, but probably not to you, given who prepares your meals."

"Remind me what Stokes looks like. I have seen his picture in the newspapers, but not recently."

"He's hard to miss. He will probably be the tallest diner in the place. I'd guess around six feet five, and he has black hair that tends to fall across his forehead, an affectation if you ask me. He probably has his barber cut it so it behaves that way. He's slender and has a long face with a pointed chin, which may really be how he got tagged as the Vulture."

"Thanks, I appreciate it."

"My pleasure. Just remember to fill me in someday. Off the record, of course, I hope that whatever is going on bodes ill for Mr. Stokes."

"I take it that he's not popular within the profession?"

Parker chuckled. "That's putting it mildly, to say the least. It's a wonder he hasn't been disbarred, given some of his outrageous performances in the courtroom. Lawyers have a bad enough reputation as it is, and Stokes just makes it worse, especially given many of his clients."

"Mobsters?"

"He has never met one of them he didn't like, or at least didn't like to defend. But I do have to say this, Archie. Despite all the histrionics, the man is good, really good. He can play a jury like a concert virtuoso plays a Stradivarius violin. I saw him in action once years ago, defending a really despicable character who deserved a life sentence, but by the time Stokes had finished describing what a terrible childhood this guy had, three of the jurors were crying—one of them a man. The defendant was found innocent after a deliberation of less than half an hour."

"Maybe Stokes hypnotized the jury," I suggested.

"In a sense, I suppose you could say he did. They certainly seemed spellbound by his closing argument. I've never seen anything like it in all my years in this profession."

"Well, I will try to avoid looking him in the eye when I meet him. Thanks for the information."

I looked up the eatery in the phone book and called, getting a stuffy-sounding man who proclaimed that I had reached "*The* Melrose Club." I asked for a one o'clock reservation for one, receiving a sniff in reply. "Just one person?" he said after the sniff as if he hadn't heard correctly.

"Does that pose a problem?"

"No, no, sir, not at all," he said, clearing his throat. "It is just that we do not often get singles during the lunch hour at the Melrose." I briefly—very briefly—considered apologizing for being me, then briefly considered suggesting that the man take a flying leap off the George Washington Bridge, but I opted to do nothing more than give him my name.

After telling Fritz I would regretfully miss his lunch, I put on a conservative suit and tie that I felt were appropriate for *The* Melrose Club. I took a taxi north to East Fifty-Fourth Street, arriving at my destination at three minutes to one. The building presented a formidable facade: windowless stone exterior, art nouveau canopy, and bronze double doors. But it lacked one of the accoutrements of any restaurant that has aspirations—a uniformed doorman.

I pushed in, turned my outerwear over to a smiling coat-check girl who had more dimples than a used golf ball, and found myself face-to-face with a tuxedoed maître d' with a grim expression. When I gave him my name, he nodded curtly, saying, "Oh yes, *the* single." I figured he would stick me next to the kitchen door, but surprisingly, I got shown to a table against one wall that gave me a clear view of the entire high-ceilinged, chandeliered room. The tables were placed discreet distances from one another, with almost all of them occupied by middle-aged men. I probably was younger than 85 percent of them.

It did not take long to spot Stokes. He sat about three tables away, in animated conversation with two others. I put his age at fifty-five, which could well mean that he dyed the black hair that fell across one side of his forehead as Nathaniel Parker had described to me.

I ordered scotch on the rocks from a friendly waiter with a warm smile who could have given lessons in civility to both the maître d' and the guy I had given my reservation to over the telephone. As I sipped my drink and perused the menu, I studied Stokes, who I had in right profile. He was doing more of the talking than his companions, and judging by his expression and their frequent nods, he was driving a point home.

When the waiter came for my lunch order, I handed him a folded sheet of white paper. "Do you know which gentleman is Mr. Stokes?" I asked, nodding in the direction of his table.

"Oh yes, sir, I certainly do. He dines with us most days; he's a regular here, a fine gentleman."

"Would you give this to him, please? He will understand."

The waiter nodded, left me, and went to Stokes's table, handing him the paper. The lawyer took it, unfolded it, frowned, and looked around the room. When his glance finally fell on me, I nodded and smiled. He did not smile, nor did I expect him to.

My filet of sole was adequate but did not measure up to Fritz's standards, which was no surprise. As I ate, I kept watching Stokes. He never again looked in my direction, but I knew I had to be on his mind. I had figured that when he and his party had finished their meal, the other two would leave and he would linger behind. I was right.

Stokes waved a good-bye to his luncheon companions and marched over to my table, where I sipped an after-meal coffee, very good coffee. Grim-faced, he glowered down at me. "I did not appreciate this," he muttered, tossing the crumpled-up note down on the table.

"Sorry, but I felt it was the best way to meet you."

"I think that you had damned well better explain yourself," Stokes demanded.

"First have a seat, and share this pot of coffee with me. They sure know how to brew it here."

"I will remain standing, thanks. Now what's all this about Nero Wolfe and Cameron Clay?"

"As I indicated in my missive, there is reason to believe that Mr. Clay was murdered."

Stokes swore. "Based on what I have read in the newspapers and heard on the air, the police do not appear to share in that belief, Mr. Goodwin."

"At the risk of my being branded a skeptic or a naysayer, the police have been known to stumble on occasion. In fact, I seem to recall numerous instances in which individuals arrested by the police and charged by the district attorney's office were later freed through the most effective courtroom work of one Roswell Stokes."

That stopped him for a second, as was intended. We were in my courtroom now, with me sitting and Stokes standing. He drew himself up to his full impressive height.

"I am not accustomed to being summoned by anyone, least of all a private detective," he huffed, trying without success to act as if he had been insulted.

"As you must know, Nero Wolfe is not just any private detective."

"I am certainly well aware that he has garnered a great deal of publicity over the years."

"Much as you have in your own field, Mr. Stokes. Why don't you sit down and have some coffee?"

The lawyer reluctantly folded his lanky frame into a chair opposite me as my smiling waiter immediately materialized. "Coffee for you, Mr. Stokes?"

"Yes, thank you very much, Raymond. Now Mr. Goodwin, just why does your boss want to see me?"

"Did you know that in the weeks before he died, Cameron Clay received a series of threatening telephone calls?"

"I did not."

"I believe it is fair to say Clay was somewhat unnerved by these calls, and he suggested five individuals who he said were the most likely to have been behind the threats."

"Only five!" Stokes roared, causing nearby diners to look our way. "Hell, that man had alienated scores of people in his columns over time."

"You were among those scores," I said. "Isn't it true that you once told a newspaper writer that 'This city has one too many newspaper columnists, and something should be done about it'?"

"I never mentioned Clay's name," Stokes said stiffly.

"Yes, but you didn't have to, did you?"

"There are several columnists whom I find distasteful."

"Okay, have it your way. I said moments ago that you were among the scores Clay had alienated. Let's narrow that: You were among the *five* Clay suspected of making threatening calls."

"Really, Mr. Goodwin," Stokes said, folding his arms across his chest. "To suggest that I would be party to such a sophomoric stunt is ludicrous."

"I am not suggesting it; Clay did. I urge you to visit Mr. Wolfe. Others among those five already have been to see him. You would be conspicuous in your refusal."

"Guilty by absence, is that it? I will not be browbeaten."

"Like you have often browbeaten witnesses?"

"I don't have to listen to this," Stokes said, making a move to rise.

"Of course, you don't, and nothing whatever is holding you here. But you might find it instructive to spend some time with Mr. Wolfe."

"Instructive? Is that a threat?"

"By no means. I am hardly in a position to threaten anyone. But you are a brilliant man, and so is Nero Wolfe. I believe you would find an evening in his company to be stimulating."

"Your attempt at flattery is transparent," he said, curling a lip.

"So I have been told by many, including several women. Just one of my numerous weaknesses."

Stokes sipped coffee and said nothing for at least a half minute. "When would Wolfe want to see me?"

"How about tonight, say nine o'clock?"

Another few seconds of silence. "Give me the address."

CHAPTER 20

I got back to the brownstone a few minutes before four, the time when Wolfe would begin his afternoon session with the orchids. "I know how you feel about lawyers, with the possible exception of Nathaniel Parker," I told him. "So you had better steel yourself, because this very evening, you will be visited by none other than the great Roswell Stokes."

"How did you manage that?"

"We just happened to have lunch today in the same restaurant, and I gave this note to the waiter to take over to Mr. Stokes." I handed Wolfe the now-crumpled note. It read:

Dear Mr. Stokes,

Nero Wolfe, the well-known private investigator, requests your presence at his office at the earliest opportunity to discuss the death of Cameron Clay and the

> *possibility that Mr. Clay was murdered. It would be to your advantage to see Mr. Wolfe before he holds a press conference.*

"Outrageous!" Wolfe roared. "I have no intention of convening a press conference, and you know it."

"Desperate times call for desperate measures."

"That proverb has been misused so often by so many that it long since ceased to have any meaning. Also, I do not consider us to be in desperate times, certainly not where Mr. Stokes is concerned."

"Well, if that's the case, I can call him and tell him not to bother coming over here tonight. . . ."

"I did not suggest that. We shall see the attorney," Wolfe said, rising and walking out of the office and toward the elevator.

We risked getting into something of a rut, hosting a visitor every night at nine. With the weekend looming, though, there would be a break before I went after the diva, Serena Sanchez, and Kerwin Andrews, the self-styled master builder and developer.

Stokes showed up right on time. I let him in and did the usual butlering in the front hall before directing him to the office. Wolfe was seated at his desk. "Mr. Stokes," he said with the hint of a nod.

"Mr. Wolfe," the lawyer said with his own slight nod as he parked himself in the red leather chair. "I suppose courtesy would dictate that I say I am happy to be here, but I have not always been known to be courteous."

"Nor have I," Wolfe said. "I have all of the simplicities, including that of brusqueness."

"Then we agree upon something," Stokes said. "With that pleasantry now out of the way, I am interested in exactly what you have to say about the death of that columnist." The last two words came out as though they were a disease.

"First, I must apologize to you, sir. I should immediately have offered you refreshments. It is a poor host indeed who imbibes while his guest's flagon remains unfilled," Wolfe said, gesturing to the beer in front of him.

"I did wonder about that," Stokes said with a thin smile, "when I noticed that well-stocked bar cart against the wall."

"Name your poison," I said, getting up to play bartender.

"Rye on the rocks, but not too many rocks," the lawyer said. While I had filled the order, Wolfe considered our guest.

"I understand Mr. Goodwin has made it known to you that Cameron Clay may have been murdered."

"Yes, he did that with all the skill of a sixth grader passing a note down the row to a friend."

"Do not be too hard on Mr. Goodwin. He is a good man, intrepid and trustworthy, but he does lack some of society's niceties, unlike you and me."

"Well said. But about Clay?"

"Yes, I digressed. I have a client who is convinced that Cameron Clay was murdered."

Stokes took a sip of his drink and nodded his approval in my direction. I scowled in return, still smarting from his "sixth grader" comment. Yet I did have the satisfaction of knowing that because of my so-called childish trick, the lawyer was right where we wanted him: sitting in the red leather chair.

Our guest turned back to Wolfe, unfazed by my scowl. "A query: Did you seek out this client, or did he come to you?"

"A fair question," Wolfe replied. "This individual sought me out. I would not have sought a commission. I had met Mr. Clay previously, and he was not someone I found in the least likable."

Stokes laughed heartily. "You and countless others. As I told Mr. Goodwin earlier today, there are scores in this town he has alienated."

"So I have learned. However, Mr. Clay felt only a handful of his detractors were likely to threaten him."

"And I am apparently said to be one of them."

"You certainly were known to bear him animus, and he wrote disparagingly about you in his column with some frequency," Wolfe said.

"Indeed he did."

"Did you ever consider legal action?"

"Not for a moment. What would it have achieved for me? I have no doubt that I could have gotten him on grounds of libel, but what price victory?"

"The great trial lawyer seen as bullying an intrepid columnist, a so-called 'man of the common people,'" Wolfe observed.

"Precisely. As many as there were who disliked—even detested—Cameron Clay, there were far more, you might term them the 'great unwashed,' who saw him as the defender of the little guy—the cabbie, the seamstress, the garbage hauler, the sales lady, the janitor, the garment worker, the longshoreman. These people and others like them were the backbone of his audience. I would have won any case I brought against Clay, but I would have been crucified in the court of public opinion."

"A pyrrhic victory."

"Hah, not even that. I would have been seen as a clear loser. I'm sure that others who Clay ripped into in his columns felt the same way about going to court. Very few suits have ever been brought against him, as you probably are aware."

"Yes, I am. I would be interested to know if you can account for your whereabouts in the early hours of—Archie, what was the date of Mr. Clay's death?" I gave it to him.

Stokes nodded and gave a tight smile. "I wondered when you were going to get to that question," he said. "I have absolutely no idea where I was, and even if I knew, I would not tell you. To think that I could have killed Cameron Clay is absolutely ludicrous."

"Perhaps, but you certainly had reason to harbor intense enmity toward the man," Wolfe said.

"No question whatever. But let us, for the sake of argument, say that I did dispatch him. How would you, or the police, or anyone else, go about proving that? If I had gone to his home with the intent of killing him, do you think I would have left fingerprints or any other proof of my presence anywhere? If I had, the police would have paid me a visit immediately. There is nothing, I repeat nothing, to tie me to his death," Stokes said, folding his arms across his chest in a gesture of self-assurance.

"Not at present," Wolfe agreed. "However, it is entirely possible that an investigation into the cause of Mr. Clay's death will be convened."

"Really? At your behest?"

"You would anoint me with authority I do not possess," Wolfe said. "But if the police do decide there is likelihood that a crime has been committed, I believe it is fair to say you will find yourself under their microscope."

"I will deal with that eventuality if and when it comes," Stokes said, still exuding confidence. "In my work, I have had many dealings with a variety of law enforcement agencies over the years. These organizations tend to use intimidation as one of their major tools, and I don't tolerate intimidation."

"Nor should you. We do not yet dwell in what I would term a police state, and I hope I do not live to see that eventuality."

"Well said, Mr. Wolfe," the lawyer replied, clapping twice.

"Have you learned what you hoped to from our meeting tonight?"

"That remains to be seen, sir. I will only say it has been an instructive evening."

"Your comment is most enigmatic, as in the old Chinese proverb 'May you live in interesting times.'"

"The source of those words may or may not have been Chinese," Wolfe said. "The origin is unknown."

"Ah, you would have been a formidable adversary in a courtroom," Stokes said good-naturedly. "I, for one, am glad you never took up law as a profession."

"As am I," Wolfe said with feeling as Stokes rose to leave. I saw him out and returned to the office.

"Well, what are your thoughts about the legendary defense attorney?" I asked Wolfe.

"Legendary, pah! Mr. Stokes is clever, without any doubt, and by all accounts extremely effective in the courtroom. But overweening pride blinds him to his shortcomings."

"Shortcomings, eh?"

"I believe he is sincere in his belief that no one he has ever encountered is as smart as he."

"Even after tonight?"

Wolfe made no comment, but it was clear to me that he felt the lawyer had met his match. As an onlooker, I agreed, but I was not about to underestimate one Roswell "The Vulture" Stokes, Esq.

CHAPTER 21

We were coming up on that long February weekend once set aside for celebrating Washington's Birthday but which had more recently become Presidents' Day so we could include Lincoln, too. As is her habit each midwinter, Lily Rowan throws a three-day bash at her place up north of the city in Katonah. She calls the retreat a "cottage," but I think *château* is a more appropriate name, given that it is three stories and has a domed swimming pool and an indoor tennis court, as well as a ballroom with a bar attached, a card room, two fireplaces, and an outdoor skating rink.

I had made arrangements months back to be in Katonah through the entire weekend, and despite the fact that we now were working on the case, Wolfe did not object. Although he is known for his aversion to women, that aversion does not extend to Lily. Ever since she asked to see his thousands of orchids years ago, he has invariably seemed pleased to see her on her visits to the brownstone.

Lily was already up at her place getting things prepared for a crowd when I steered the Heron sedan north in a snowfall on Friday afternoon. I turned in the long driveway that led to Chez Rowan and was met by the chatelaine herself as I pulled up in front of the four-car garage.

"Escamillo, you are prompt as usual," she said, clapping her hands gleefully. "Come with me and have a hot chocolate. Leave your car where it is. Charles will bring your baggage in and put the car away. Heaven forbid it should get covered with any more snow than it already has." Charles is Lily's longtime butler-chauffeur. I obeyed orders, and ten minutes later, we sat sipping chocolate in front of a stone fireplace with a roaring blaze.

"I have assembled quite a guest list," she said proudly. "You will have met many of them before, including one woman who is simply dying to have you as her bridge partner."

"Is she any good?"

"Not bad, based on the two or three times that we've played together. Not as good as you are, of course, but I doubt if anyone who is coming can match you at Mr. Goren's game."

"Flattery will get you everywhere with me, et cetera, et cetera. Will all your guests be staying over?"

"All but a few who live nearby. That's the benefit of having a place with all these bedrooms. I've lost count of the number, but I think it's fourteen, or maybe fifteen. There is one guest you will be particularly interested in meeting."

"Really? Well, please don't keep me in suspense."

"It is none other than Serena Sanchez."

I set my mug of chocolate down. "Now that is a surprise."

"I'm sure you will like her. She can be quite the charmer, so just make sure that you don't end up liking her too much."

"I will try to control myself."

"I'm sure that you will. She seemed quite interested in meeting a real live private detective."

"Does that mean I have to wear a trench coat with the collar pulled up and a snap-brim fedora?"

"I think one of those glen plaid sports coats of yours will do just fine."

"Just how does Miss Sanchez happen to be here?"

Lily first answered with a sly grin, followed by a chuckle. "One, I thought our guests would be interested in having a noted diva among their number and might even ask her to sing; two, I know you and Nero Wolfe are looking into the death of Cameron Clay; three, Serena Sanchez once was married to Clay; and four, I figured that at some point you and Wolfe might want to talk to Serena and that I could help that process along. Or . . . have you spoken to her already?"

"No, although for your ears only, that happens to be on our schedule."

"Excellent!" she said. "See, I'm helping do your work. You should be proud of me. And I am positive you will find Serena both charming and totally innocent in the death of that not-very-nice man."

"I am always proud of you," I said, "even if you sometimes are a bit eager in taking the bull by the horns."

"And we both know something about bulls, don't we, Escamillo? Just think: If there hadn't been that angry bull in a pasture years ago, we might never have met. And wouldn't that have been a shame?"

"I won't for a single minute deny that, my love."

Cocktails Friday night began at five sharp, to the sound of a gong, no less. The guests had been arriving all afternoon, many in limousines, others by taxi from the Katonah railroad station, and a few in their own cars. At Lily's earlier suggestion, I donned a glen plaid sport coat and brown slacks, along with a tan shirt and a burgundy tie.

By the time I reached the ballroom, it was crowded, with many of the guests clustered at the bar, although two red bow-tie wearing waitresses also circulated with trays of champagne and martinis. Scanning the multitude, I recognized several people from other parties Lily had thrown in her duplex and out here, where her summer weekend parties are every bit as elaborate as this winter extravaganza.

I started for the bar when a slender arm encircled mine. "Hello, big boy, can I hang on to you?" Lily said.

"Certainly, but only if you allow me to order you a drink. Do you approve of my attire?"

"Of course, I do. You are without doubt the best-dressed—and best-looking—man in the room."

"If what you say is true, and modesty forbids me to comment, then it is only fitting that I am at this moment in the company of the best-dressed, best-looking woman here."

"We're both pretty full of ourselves, aren't we?" Lily said with a smug smile as we each got a scotch and water from the bartender. "Ah, look at who is joining this august gathering." She nodded toward a slender and exotic brunette who had just entered the room on the arm of a plain, sandy-haired fellow.

"That, my dear, is Serena Sanchez," Lily said. "What do you think?"

"Attractive, curvaceous, self-possessed, for starters. Somehow, I thought she would be older."

"At the risk of sounding catty, and I really don't mean to,

she is older than she looks, but she has got wonderful bone structure. Let's go over there. I want you to meet her.

"Serena, I am so glad you could come," Lily said, holding out a hand.

"I was delighted to receive your invitation," the diva said in only the slightest Spanish accent. "I would like you to meet William Phelps, who is an official with the Metropolitan Opera."

"If you call a public relations man an official, I suppose I qualify," Phelps said with a smile and a blush, bowing slightly to Lily.

"And I would like you both to meet my friend Archie Goodwin," Lily said. I shook Phelps's paw and took Serena's hand, resisting the temptation to kiss it.

"Ah, I am happy to meet the famous private detective," she said with a dazzling smile. "Lily has told me much about you, every bit of it good."

"I'm afraid Miss Rowan is too kind. I am not a famous detective, but I work for a famous one."

"Well, Archie is famous in my book," Lily said, turning toward Serena. "When I told some of my other guests you would be here, they asked if you might sing for us. I made no promises, because I didn't know if you would want to perform. That is definitely not the reason I invited you here for the weekend."

"I would be honored to sing one aria, perhaps a little later?"

"Absolutely. We won't be eating until seven. Please get drinks and hors d'oeuvres and enjoy yourselves."

Lily and I spent the next half hour moving through the crowd, with her making introductions. She is a master at working a room, and she played her role as the gracious and charming hostess to the hilt. I was proud to be with her—as usual.

We then separated and I wandered through the room, talking to a few people I had met at Lily's before, including a fine-arts dealer who had once hired Wolfe to find out who in his gallery had been dipping into the till. We ended up catching the woman, who had seemed to be the least likely suspect among the four employees.

I was jawing with an advertising creative director who recently had won an award for a television commercial for potato chips when Lily clapped her hands twice, causing the nattering throughout the room to quickly die down.

"Attention, everyone. One of our guests, who some of you already have had the privilege to meet tonight, is Serena Sanchez, the great international mezzo-soprano who has sung numerous times right here in New York with the Met and is famed for her portrayal as Carmen. She will sing one aria from that great opera. I am proud to introduce . . . Serena Sanchez."

Applause followed, lots of it. Serena smiled broadly and talked to the piano player seated at a Steinway against the wall. He nodded and smiled, and she turned to the guests, who had crowded in.

"I am going to sing the "Habanera" from *Carmen*, which I know many of you will recognize. For this, I will need a man, as I always sing it with a man close to me, very close." That drew scattered laughter, including from me, although what she said next put a stop to my laugh.

"Mr. Archie Goodwin, will you kindly agree to be my consort for this aria? I understand you have been called 'Escamillo,' which is most fitting, because he is one of the principals in the opera, and a lover of Carmen."

I stepped forward reluctantly, getting something of an applause myself. "Now, Escamillo, stand there while I begin." She motioned to a spot a few feet from her.

Feeling something of the fool, I was rooted to the spot while she began to sing as the piano played, and what singing it was! She burst forth in sultry tones that captivated the crowd—and me. "Are you a good dancer, Archie Goodwin?" she asked between bars.

"Depends on who you ask."

"Serena, he is a very good dancer," Lily chimed in.

"Then watch this and do it with me," the diva said before starting to sing again. She went into a series of steps that I later learned was a *habanera*, the same word as the aria. I picked up on it, and she grinned, moving toward me with a long scarf that she looped around my waist, pulling me to her. Then we began dancing belly to belly as she sang the song I had remembered hearing when Lily and I went to the Met.

We moved together, and then she would push off from me and twirl, but never stop singing. To call her dancing sensuous would be an understatement. We went on for several minutes, time seemed not to matter, and when she pushed off one last time and twirled with her hands above her head, the audience clapped, whistled, and erupted with "bravas." Serena bowed to me and then in the direction of the pianist. I bowed back, feeling much less like a fool than I had earlier.

"You did very well, Archie Goodwin," she said. "Better than many of the singers I have danced with in opera houses. A good singer is not always a good dancer."

"Just never ask me to sing," I said, drawing a hearty laugh from her and from the crowd.

"I probably should have warned you that she had that planned," Lily said later when we were at the bar. "But I figured you could handle it, and you did."

"She's quite the all-around performer. Does she still do a lot of operas?"

"No, not so much anymore, or so she's told me. She feels her voice is beginning to go, so she's cut way back on appearances."

"You could have fooled me. I'm far from an expert, but I thought she sounded terrific."

"Serena is her own harshest critic," Lily said. "She doesn't want to be seen as a once-great star who stays at the party too long. She is very sensitive about that, and about what she views as her diminished talents. But sing no sad songs for her. She is enjoying teaching now, giving master classes and working with operatic hopefuls. She says she finds it very rewarding."

"Any men in her life?"

"Not that I'm aware of. That fellow she came with is just a long-time friend who comes in handy as an escort when she's in New York."

"Where's home for her, Spain?"

"Not any longer. She's got a house in Connecticut, which makes it easy for her to come into the city. I really believe she would like to do more at Juilliard."

"Well, now that we've danced together, I wonder how she will react when I tell her Nero Wolfe wants to talk to her about her ex-husband's death."

"I think she'll be just fine with that. In fact, I know she will."

"Why is that?"

"Because, my dear Escamillo, I have already told her to expect an invitation to visit Mr. Wolfe."

The rest of the weekend was uneventful and pleasant. You might think because of what Lily had told Serena Sanchez, there would be awkwardness between us, but there wasn't. On Saturday afternoon, with light snow falling, the diva and I skated on the rink along with a half dozen other couples, and we also were seated together at dinner that night and engaged in what I would call amicable conversation. She did not raise the subject of a visit to Wolfe, nor did I. There would be time for that.

"Serena seems quite taken with you," Lily said later, "which does not surprise me in the least, given your charm. I suppose I should be jealous."

"You have no reason to be. By the way, you have no shortage of admirers yourself. I had a hard time getting to dance with you, what with all those swains lined up ahead of me."

"Swains? What an interesting word. Did you pick that up from Nero Wolfe?"

"Don't you think I have a vocabulary of my own?"

"Oops, I didn't mean to hit a sore spot. Of course, I know you have a way with words, you silver-tongued rascal. And I understand you also made quite a hit at the bridge table last night, bringing home a small slam, doubled, no less. At least two ladies were most impressed with that feat, and they talked about nothing else at breakfast."

"I do what I can to keep your friends amused."

"Just as long as they are not *too* amused."

"Point taken. Do you have a phone number where I can reach Serena in New York? For purely professional reasons, of course."

"Of course. While she's conducting that master class at Juilliard, she's staying at the Churchill," Lily said, pulling an address book from her purse and flipping it open. "Room 806. As I said earlier, she will not be surprised to hear from you regarding a visit to see Nero Wolfe."

"Has she mentioned anything about Clay's death to you?"

"Only to say she felt no emotions of any kind when she learned he was dead. If you want my vote, it is that Serena had nothing whatever to do with what happened to her ex-husband."

"I always want your vote, and I will pass your thoughts along to Mr. Wolfe."

"I wouldn't bother if I were you. I can't imagine that Nero Wolfe would ever take an opinion of mine seriously."

"That's where you are wrong, my dear. He thinks very highly of you."

"I'm not sure I believe you, but it's nice to hear anyway."

Several people left Katonah Sunday afternoon, including Serena and her consort, William Phelps of the Metropolitan Opera Company. I said my good-byes to her at the front door as Phelps loaded their bags into a waiting limousine.

"It has been very nice making your acquaintance, Archie Goodwin," Serena said, standing on tiptoe and kissing me on the cheek. "And I understand that your employer, the famous Nero Wolfe, is wanting to see me about the death of my former husband. I look forward to speaking with him. Will you be present?"

I said I would, which landed me another kiss on the cheek. As the limo pulled away, I turned back to the house, where Lily was waiting in the doorway. "Not one kiss but two. Whatever am I to do with you?"

"I've often wondered that. I guess it's fair to say that my charm is also my curse."

"Ah, so that's what it is? Well, even though some of the folks have departed, there are lots of us left, and tonight we will be dancing to the music of a six-piece band I've brought in from Poughkeepsie that is said to be quite popular with the girls over at Vassar and their dates. I expect to have the first dance, the last dance, and several in-between with you."

"I find nothing whatever to object to in that statement," I said. "Let us show the folks here how it's done."

As it turned out, Lily and I were impressive on the dance

floor that night, if I do say so myself. But as good a time as I was having, I couldn't help but think about Serena Sanchez and how the lady would react to meeting and being grilled by Nero Wolfe.

CHAPTER 22

By the time I got to the brownstone Monday night after dropping Lily off at her penthouse, I was too tired to report to Wolfe, so I went straight upstairs to my room, bypassing the office.

At breakfast the next morning in the kitchen, Fritz wanted to hear the details of the weekend. He had been at the Katonah retreat himself several years earlier to supervise the preparation of a feast for a hundred or so guests at one of Lily's charity fund-raisers.

I filled him in on our activities, although he was far more interested in hearing about the new, top-of-the-line range and refrigerator Lily recently had installed at Katonah. He had been urging Wolfe to get new kitchen appliances for years, and this information would no doubt spur him on.

At my desk in the office, I found bills that needed paying and orchid records to be entered on file cards, but no notes from Wolfe. He came down from the plant rooms at eleven and, after placing a raceme of orange *Laelia* in his desk vase, he rang for beer and asked if I had enjoyed the long weekend.

"Very much," I replied. "Miss Rowan sends you her warm greetings. And lest you think I did not devote at least some of my time in Katonah to work, I made the acquaintance of one of the other guests, Serena Sanchez."

He raised his eyebrows. "Did you bewitch her?"

"Only to the extent that I often bewitch beautiful women. While she was under my spell, Miss Sanchez agreed to come to the brownstone and talk to you about Cameron Clay."

If Wolfe was pleased, he chose not to show it, concentrating instead on uncapping one of the two chilled bottles of Remmers beer that Fritz had just placed before him along with a pilsner glass.

"When would you like to see Miss Sanchez?" I asked. "She is expecting a call from me."

"Tonight," he grumbled, realizing he would have to go back to work sooner than he had anticipated.

"She is teaching a master class in voice at the Juilliard, so I might not be able to reach her until later," I told him. "But when I told her you wanted to meet with her, she was agreeable."

That did not impress Wolfe, who, after his first sip of beer, had riffled through the day's mail I had stacked on his blotter. He found nothing of interest in the mail and opened his current book, *84, Charing Cross Road*, by Helene Hanff.

To hell with it, I thought; maybe I could catch a break and reach the lady at home. I dialed the Churchill Hotel and asked for her room. To my surprise, she answered.

"Hello, Serena."

"I recognize that voice," she said with a laugh. "It is Archie

Goodwin, the great dancer, is it not? And you are, of course, calling to invite me to meet your Mr. Nero Wolfe. I shall endeavor to make myself available."

"Would it be inconvenient for you to come to Mr. Wolfe's home tonight?"

There was a pause at the other end. "No, I could come. When would you like me to be there?"

"What about nine o'clock?" I gave her the address.

"That is good. And I will be on time, Archie."

"I would never doubt that for a second," I told her. "But to make things easier for you, I can arrange to have a taxi pick you up at the Churchill and then take you back home when you leave here. The driver is an old friend of mine named Herb Aronson, who has been helpful to us for years. If you don't hear from me in the next half hour, Mr. Aronson will be at the front entrance of the hotel at eight forty-five." I gave her the number of Herb's cab.

"That is most gracious of you, Archie." After hanging up with Serena, I called Herb's home number, knowing he was usually off-duty at this hour of the morning.

"Hey, Private Cop, I haven't heard from you in days, maybe weeks. Is it something about my driving style, or did you just decide to stop riding in hacks?"

"None of the above, cab jockey. In fact, I have a round-trip fare for you tonight, and one that I think you'll really enjoy."

"I'm all ears."

"I happen to know you are a fan of opera, and your passenger tonight will be a prima donna, Serena Sanchez."

"Damn! I saw her at the Met in *Carmen* six or seven years back. She's the real goods. Lead me to her."

I gave Herb the particulars, and he sounded as excited as a high school sophomore learning he was getting a date with the homecoming queen.

"Miss Sanchez will be here at nine tonight, per your instructions," I said to Wolfe, who showed no reaction, other than to sigh. Once again he would have to go to work.

Serena was on time, which did not surprise me, given Herb Aronson's efficiency. He even escorted the diva to our front door, tipping his cap to her. "I will be right here at the curb the whole time you are inside," he said, "ready to take you back to the Churchill."

"You are too kind," she replied, giving him a wide smile as she stepped into the front hall. "What a nice man," she told me as I helped her off with her sable coat. "He said he had seen me perform at the Met. Do you think he was truthful, or just flattering me?"

"I happen to know that he was truthful. Would I select just any driver to chauffeur a famous Carmen? Mr. Aronson loves the opera and goes often, and when I mentioned your name to him, he was absolutely enthralled."

At that, Serena, who I could tell loved flattery, actually blushed and smiled shyly, showing her dimples. As I led her down the hall to the office, I hoped she was not the one who had sent Cameron Clay to his final reward.

"Good evening," she said to Nero Wolfe, who looked up from his book and gave his usual dip of the chin.

"Madam," he said as she slid into the red leather chair at the end of his desk, "would you like something to drink?"

"Do you have sherry?" she asked as she crossed one nyloned leg over the other. They were good legs, and her skirt was short enough to show them off. I wondered if Lily Rowan had told her of Wolfe's admiration for a well-turned gam. I made a mental note to ask her.

I handed Serena a glass of sherry, and she took a delicate sip, nodding her approval. "You wish to see me because you think that I killed my former husband," she said to Wolfe. I could tell he was surprised by her frontal attack.

"You come straight to the point," he replied.

"I see no reason to waste your valuable time, Mr. Wolfe. In truth, I have been expecting someone to accuse me of killing Cameron, and much to my surprise, no one has—until now."

"I accuse you of nothing," Wolfe said. "I am conducting an investigation on behalf of a client who is of the opinion that Mr. Clay was murdered. I have come to no conclusion."

"From what I understand and have read, the police say he committed suicide."

"That is their position. Have they spoken to you?"

"Yes, but only very briefly. They asked if I could account for my time on the night—or really the early morning—when Cameron apparently had been shot."

"And could you account for your time?"

"No, not for all of it. I had been at a party with a number of members of the Metropolitan Opera at a restaurant, and it went on quite late. I am afraid I had more to drink than I should have, so to clear my head, I walked the several blocks to the Churchill, as it was quite a mild evening for February. And when I got to the hotel, I don't recall anyone seeing me come in."

"Not even an elevator operator?"

"The elevators there are now self-operated, I am sorry to say. I liked the old way better, with those nice, friendly men in uniforms taking you up and down."

"Do you believe Mr. Clay killed himself?"

Serena shrugged. "I really don't know. It has been a few years since I have seen him, and he may have changed. Based on the things he had said about me in his column since we were divorced, though, he seemed like the same nasty man I came to know in our last days together. Why he would want to kill himself, I can't imagine. I suppose you never met Cameron?"

"I did meet him, madam, but only once."

"One time should have been enough for you to see the type of individual he was."

"So I have heard from others. Do you own a firearm?" Wolfe asked.

She rolled her eyes. "That always comes back to haunt me. I suppose that you are referring to the time many years ago that I shot a man in Madrid."

"I am, although I realize that stories, as they are retold, often become altered, sometimes beyond recognition. I would like to hear your version of the events."

She squared her shoulders, as if she were about to begin a recitation in a classroom. "I was young, not quite twenty, and I was beginning to make my way in the operatic world in my native country of Spain. I started noticing a man who was attending all of my performances, sitting in one of the front rows. His eyes were always on me, even when I was not singing.

"Then he would wait after the opera and try to talk to me. He even tried to hand me a bouquet of roses once, but the guard at the stage door stopped him when he saw that I did not want the flowers. Next, he started following me on the streets of the city. He found out where I lived and would wait for me and try to talk to me when I stepped outside. That is when I purchased a pistol through a friend."

"With the intent of shooting him?" I asked.

"No, not at all, just as—what would you call it?—as something to discourage him if he became too persistent."

"But the gun was loaded," Wolfe said.

She nodded, soberly. "That was a mistake, but my friend, the one who got it for me, said I needed bullets in case something happened. And something did happen. The man who had been following me came right up to me one night on a street near where I lived. He grabbed me and started trying to kiss me. I broke away and he ran after me. I pulled the pistol from my purse and shot him in the leg. He screamed and fell down on the pavement, yelling and holding on to the leg.

"I started screaming myself, but screaming for the police to come. People came out of their homes to see what had happened, and soon the police did arrive, along with an ambulance that took the man to a hospital. I got taken away to their headquarters, and eventually, I went before a magistrate, I think he was called. I was already making good money with my singing, so I hired a very good lawyer, who learned that the man I shot had been in trouble before for attacking women. I was released with a warning, and I had to surrender the pistol. That was all right with me, because I was done forever with guns. I have never even held one since then."

"However, you have threatened Cameron Clay," Wolfe said.

"Only in anger. After our divorce, we have run into each other several times, I am sorry to say. Once, a year or so ago, we both were in the same restaurant here, and that was just after he had said some insulting things about me in his column. When I saw him, I shouted at him."

"Is it true that you said 'I will kill you'?" I asked.

She exhaled and nodded. "Yes, yes, I did say that, but I was not serious. I do have a temper. That much is true. Others will tell you that about me. Too often, I say things I do not mean."

Wolfe drank beer and set his glass down. "When is the last time you saw Mr. Clay?"

"It was that very night, in that restaurant. I never laid eyes on him again, that is the Lord's truth, although he continued to write hurtful things about me in his newspaper."

"Madam, I believe you have a taxi waiting for you. Archie will see you out," Wolfe said, rising and walking out of the office.

Serena turned to me with a puzzled expression. "Is Mr. Wolfe angry with me? Did I say something I shouldn't have?"

"No, he is that way. He does not waste time on small talk. He felt there was nothing more to be said."

I helped Serena with her coat, and we went outside and down the steps to Herb's waiting cab. "Get this fine lady home safely," I told him, handing him some bills to cover both the round-trip fare and the waiting time.

"I should pay him myself, Archie," Serena said, reaching into her handbag.

"No you should not; this one is on me," I told her. "After all, when we were up at Lily's place in Katonah, you taught me the *habanera*. Now I have something new that I can use to show off with on the dance floor."

She laughed. "You are a quick learner, Archie Goodwin."

"I try to be. Now let Mr. Aronson ask you more about your opera career. He is a good listener, and I'm sure you have many more wonderful stories that he would be delighted to hear." I waved as they pulled away from the curb, with Herb grinning and looking over his shoulder adoringly at his famous and glamorous passenger.

CHAPTER 23

"Would you care to comment?" I asked Wolfe when I got back inside and he had returned to his desk chair, free from the presence of a female in the brownstone.

"The woman is most self-possessed."

"Probably comes from all those years of performing. Do you think she is capable of murder?"

"Assuredly."

"Yet she came to see you without the least bit of complaining or reluctance."

"As you said, she is a performer. How best to deflect suspicion than to appear eager to cooperate with one's interrogators."

"That sounds cynical," I told him.

"Cynical? No, realistic," Wolfe said. "But you are the expert on the vagaries of the female of the species. Once again, I should be questioning you about her."

"Ah, you want to know if I think she killed him. I'd give long odds against, say seven to one, maybe seven to two."

"I asked earlier if you had bewitched her. Has *she* bewitched *you*?"

"That is a fair question, and my answer is no. An attractive woman? Absolutely. A shrewd one? Yes again. Someone I would like to develop a serious relationship with? No . . . in capital letters. I am not drawn to mercurial women. They simply take more effort than I am willing to expend. But is she a killer? No . . . despite her antics with a pistol in Spain many years ago. That is my take on her. Do we talk to the developer next?"

"Mr. Andrews, yes," Wolfe said.

"May I assume you want to see the gentleman—and I could be using the term loosely—as soon as possible?"

"You may."

"These nine o'clock séances are getting to be a habit. I will do what I can to deliver him to you with dispatch."

The next morning after breakfast, I telephoned Lon Cohen. "Any success involving the case of the dead columnist?" he asked.

"We are hard at work, of course. But I need a favor."

"Of course, you do. What else is new?"

"At present, and this is not for publication, Wolfe has talked to four of the five individuals Clay seemed to fear most. That leaves Kerwin Andrews."

"The self-styled master builder. What do you need from me?"

"I'm trying to figure out how to approach him. Any suggestions?"

"Let me talk to our real-estate writer. He knows Andrews, of course, how could he not? The man is a publicity hound, sending out press releases by the scores. I'll get back to you."

I had not heard from Lon by the time Wolfe came down at eleven, and I was about to tell him of my lack of progress when the doorbell rang. I went down the hall and saw the bulky figure on the stoop through the one-way glass.

"Cramer," I told Wolfe back in the office. "Do I admit him?"

"Yes," he muttered as the doorbell continued to sound.

"Sorry to keep you waiting, we were in conference," I told the inspector, who tramped in without speaking and marched down the hall to the office.

"Good morning, sir," Wolfe said. "Would you like some coffee? I realize you do not imbibe this early in the day."

"Nothing for me," Cramer grunted, settling into the red leather chair. "I dropped by to see how you're doing with your Cameron Clay investigation."

"I am mildly surprised at your interest. I thought you and the department had firmly settled on suicide as the cause of death."

"I'm still convinced of that, but we, specifically Humbert, are feeling some heat from the folks at the *Gazette*. Me, I don't much give a damn about what the newspaper people think—that's off the record—but the commissioner spends a lot of time worrying about his image—also off the record. So in a nutshell, that's why I'm here."

"I have nothing of substance to report to you," Wolfe said. "Archie and I are still at work. I do have a question, however."

"That's typical," Cramer said. "You've got nothing for me, but I'm asked to fork over what I have to you."

"My request is modest, sir. Have you talked to Mr. McNeil, the columnist's assistant?"

"Yeah, and McNeil's clean, if that's what you're asking. He said he was at a bachelor party during the overnight period when Clay died, and he gave us the names of the other guys who he was getting loaded with. They corroborated his story, all six of them."

"It would be difficult to get that number of persons to lie for you," Wolfe commented.

"That's what we thought, too, not that we ever suspected him. Anything else you want to know?"

"No, sir. If I come to a conclusion regarding Mr. Clay's death, you will be informed."

"Well, I am certainly glad to hear that!" Cramer snapped, rising. "It's always nice to know that you are thinking of the department." He walked out without another word.

"The inspector is not a happy man," I said when I got back to the office after locking the front door behind him, "but that is hardly anything new."

Wolfe started to reply but he was cut short by the telephone's jangle. "Archie, this is your lucky day," Lon Cohen said.

"I'm delighted to hear that, news hawk. Did I win the Irish Sweepstakes?"

"Even better. You have a chance to meet the great Kerwin Andrews this very afternoon."

"Great, eh? To what do I owe this opportunity?"

"The developer himself is holding a press conference at three o'clock to announce a big new multiuse development along the East River. Stores, offices, apartments, restaurants, in a six-building complex, with one tower to be fifty-five stories. His latest hyperbolic press release calls it the 'most-extensive project to be undertaken in Manhattan since the construction of Rockefeller Center.'"

"I feel I should genuflect, even though I'm not a churchgoer with any regularity. Do I need press credentials to attend this gathering?"

"Yes, but that has been taken care of. You will be present,

representing the *Gazette*, along with our real-estate guy, Chuck Miller."

"How will I know him?"

"Don't worry. Chuck knows what you look like. Your picture's been in the *Gazette* enough times."

"I knew that fame would eventually pay off in some small way. Tell me where to be." Lon spelled out the details, and I filled Wolfe in. He nodded and went back to reading his book. If he was pleased, he managed to hide it well.

At ten minutes to three, I stood along the East River with several dozen other shivering people who were braving the gusty winds off the water. Chuck Miller did recognize me and gave me a plastic pin-on card that identified me as A. GOODWIN, *NEW YORK GAZETTE*. "Just put this on your coat, Archie, although it's not really necessary," Miller said. "If Andrews had his way, the whole town would turn out to hear his priceless orations, whether or not they're from the press. Like a politician, he has never met a crowd he didn't like."

"An oversize ego?"

"Large economy size is more like it. Speak of the devil, here the great man comes."

Kerwin Andrews stepped out of a limo and waved to the gathering. He was clad in a black overcoat and sported a neatly trimmed salt-and-pepper beard. I recognized him from newspaper photographs, much as Chuck Miller had recognized me in the same way. So we both were celebrities of a sort, but separated by a net worth of a few million dollars.

"Thank you all for coming here on this grand occasion," Andrews boomed in a voice that could easily be heard on the Long Island City side of the river, although no one over on that bank seemed to be listening. "As a third-generation New Yorker,

I am proud of my great city and my heritage, and I am also proud to be introducing this enterprise, which I honestly believe will transform this underdeveloped area. The plans have been drawn up, and they will be on display later in the boathouse over there"—he gestured to a squat building behind him—"but before we look at those plans, I want you all to remember that the spot where we are all now standing will one day be the cornerstone of what will become known as . . . Andrews Point!"

A few of Andrews's underlings, at least I assumed that's what they were, began clapping vigorously. Soon, others in the assemblage followed suit, with the possible exception of some members of the press, who rarely clapped for anyone or anything. I joined these journalists in withholding judgment.

Andrews droned on for several more minutes about his love of New York, told a lame joke or two to show that he was just one of the common people, and then waved us toward the boathouse where he promised we would learn more about Andrews Point. Like lemmings, we followed him, happy to be out of the weather.

Inside the low-ceilinged, oak-beamed building, we were greeted by waiters serving drinks and a table in the center of the room with a model of Andrews's project. I politely turned down a drink and headed for the model, which displayed a series of interconnected buildings along the river in miniature, finely detailed and with tiny people positioned on a promenade along the river. An idyllic setting.

"Damned impressive, isn't it?" came a smooth voice from over my shoulder. It was the developer himself. "I don't believe I know you," Kerwin Andrews said, grinning and holding out a hand, which I shook. "You are"—he peered at my name tag—"Mr. Goodwin of the *Gazette*. Glad that you are here today. You must work with Mr. Miller."

"Actually, I work with Nero Wolfe. You may have heard of him."

Never have I seen an expression change so quickly. One moment, Andrews wore a triumphant look, the next, an unsure and puzzled one.

"I don't believe I understand," he said, lowering his voice as his eyes moved around the room to see if anyone was within earshot.

"So you have heard of Nero Wolfe?"

He nodded, still clearly off balance. "What, if anything, does this have to do with me?"

"Mr. Wolfe is investigating the death of Cameron Clay, and he would like very much to talk to you."

"Now, you listen to me," Andrews said in what I would describe as a loud whisper, "I don't know what your game is, Mr. Goodwin, but I am not going to play it. I could have you thrown out of here."

"You could," I agreed, "but that would hardly be wise. This is a triumphant moment for you. You've got the press, TV, cameras, and radio gathered, even our deputy mayor over there with a glass of champagne in his hand, if I am not mistaken. The last thing you need now is a distraction.

"You should be mixing with all of these people, working the room, and I'll stay in the background until things begin to break up. Then we will talk."

That did the trick. Andrews turned away from me as if we had been having a friendly conversation and strode toward a gaggle of invitees who were admiring the model of his ambitious new project. He began shaking hands and describing the advantages of what he referred to as this "self-contained city within a city, in which one can live, work, shop, exercise, eat, and drink without ever having to step outside to brave the kind of weather we are having right here today."

The party went on for more than an hour, climaxing when Andrews took a portable microphone and further extolled the benefits of his "nirvana on the river" as flashbulbs popped and TV cameras recorded the moment.

"To make way for all of this, won't many people and businesses be uprooted?" a reporter from the *Daily News* posed.

"I am glad you asked that," Andrews said, his smile showing off a set of pearly whites that may have been manufactured. "Our team has done extensive studies showing that a minimum of people and enterprises will be displaced. As most of you know, the immediate area here has been in decline for years," he said with a sweep of the hand.

"No one now resides in the three square blocks around us, except, of course, vagrants who panhandle, accosting what few passersby there are on these almost deserted streets. The former tenements and shops are boarded up, and the city inspectors have found many of them to be rat-infested."

That brought a smattering of applause, followed by bland questions from a few individuals who seemed suspiciously like plants. Andrews fielded these softballs with an ease that suggested he was expecting each of them. The guy was glib, I'll give him that, oily but glib.

As the party began breaking up and the TV crews packed their gear, Andrews increasingly looked in my direction and finally walked over to me, making sure we were well out of earshot.

"All right, Mr. Goodwin, you had better tell me what this is all about and tell me fast," he said, gritting those too-perfect teeth of his.

"As I told you, Mr. Wolfe is investigating the death of Cameron Clay. Although the police have said it appears to be a suicide, there is reason to believe Mr. Clay may have been murdered."

"And as I asked you earlier, what does this have to do with me?"

"In the days before he died, Clay began receiving telephone calls that contained death threats. He identified five people who might be behind those threats. You were one of them."

"Outrageous!" Andrews stormed, trying without success to keep his voice down.

"Mr. Wolfe has been hired to determine whether there is reason to believe Cameron Clay was murdered. He already has talked to the other four persons the columnist had suspected of making those calls, and now he would like to see you."

"Well, I'll be damned if I am going to humor him," Andrews said, although his act of bravado had begun to waver.

"Suit yourself, Mr. Andrews, although when Mr. Wolfe is quoted in the press, as is almost certain to occur, he will, in all probability, mention your refusal to sit down with him."

"I don't for a single minute believe that your Nero Wolfe is going to say one damned word to the press about me," Andrews snapped. "I know he does not covet the attention of the newspapers, but rather avoids the spotlight."

"Are you willing to take the gamble that Mr. Wolfe won't on this occasion talk to the newspapers? He can be unpredictable."

"I had absolutely nothing to do with Clay's death, nothing. Period. End of discussion."

"Then you also have nothing to fear from a conversation with Nero Wolfe. Mr. Andrews, this is hardly the time for you to receive bad publicity, whether or not it is merited," I said. "You stand on the threshold of an epic project, one which promises to remake a section of Manhattan desperately in need of revitalization, as you so eloquently described to us just minutes ago in this very room. Will you jeopardize that opportunity by refusing to see my boss?"

"This amounts to outright blackmail," he fumed.

"I don't think so, sir."

"Who are those other four people that you say he has talked to?"

"Uh-uh, Mr. Andrews. That is confidential, just as your visit with him will be. Or don't you care whether people know about it?"

"Dammit, when does he want to see me?"

"Tonight, at his office."

"Tonight! What if I happen to have other plans?"

"I would strongly advise you to alter them."

Andrews's self-confidence—some might term it arrogance—had deserted him, which was not a pretty sight. "All right," he said, exhaling, "give me the time and place."

CHAPTER 24

When Wolfe came down from the plant rooms at six, I was able to tell him Kerwin Andrews would be paying a visit to us three hours later. "And he was not in the least happy about it," I said.

"How did you threaten him?" Wolfe asked as he rang for beer.

"I suggested that, because he is about to undertake a colossal real estate development, the last thing he needs at this time is bad publicity. I also hinted that you might go to the press and mention his refusal to talk to you, but he didn't buy that."

He frowned. "I do not condone your methods, and you got something of a comeuppance."

"Well, I am sure sorry to hear that you feel that way, but you have tasked me with delivering five people to you for questioning. This I have done, assuming Kerwin Andrews shows up here tonight, and I have twenty dollars that says he will be ringing our doorbell at nine. It is true that I have employed a variety of means to get these various individuals to the brownstone, some of the means not to your liking, but I have broken no laws, nor have I endangered the private investigator's license issued to me by the sovereign State of New York."

Wolfe glowered at me. "Are you quite through?"

"I am."

"Good. *Tasked* is not a verb in this house," he said.

"It is when I am talking," I shot back. Wolfe was fuming, but I knew him well enough to realize he was not in a position to complain too much. He knew exactly what he was getting lo those many years ago when he hired me to be a burr under his saddle and to use whatever means—within reason, of course—to fulfill his wishes when we were on a case.

Wolfe was still a little hot under the collar during dinner, but that didn't stop him from expounding on the reasons why the Union general George Meade was smarter than Confederate general Robert E. Lee at the Battle of Gettysburg during the Civil War. As was often the case during these mealtime talks, it was a one-sided affair, with him talking and me nodding and chewing. At least it kept us from each other's throat.

When we went back in the office with coffee, the minutes seemed to crawl, and I felt a sense of relief when the front bell sounded promptly at nine. I opened the door to a somber Kerwin Andrews, who glowered at me and stepped in without uttering a word. After I hung up his coat and hat, I led him to the office, also without a word on my part.

"You are Nero Wolfe," he announced to my boss as I directed him to the red leather chair.

"I am, sir. Will you have something to drink?"

"You're damn right I will. I've been strong-armed into coming here tonight, and the least you can do is make it less painful."

"Indeed? Did Mr. Goodwin exert physical force upon you?"

"Of course not, you know what I mean. I'll have scotch and soda."

"You also know why I want to speak to you," Wolfe said as I mixed Andrews's drink on the bar cart.

"According to Goodwin here, you seem to think that swine Cameron Clay was murdered."

"If that is what he told you, I regret to say he misspoke," Wolfe said. "I have been hired to find out *whether* Mr. Clay was killed."

"Who hired you?"

"That information is not germane to our discussion."

"So you say," Andrews replied, taking a sip of his drink. "My understanding from everything I have read and heard is that the New York City Police feel Clay did away with himself."

"Yes, that is clearly their position."

"So what makes you think otherwise?"

"In the last weeks of his life, Mr. Clay said he received numerous threatening telephone calls."

"I find that hardly surprising, given the way he alienated people in print over the years."

"It is true that he made many enemies, you among them," Wolfe said.

"I don't deny it for a minute."

"I would hardly expect you to. You brought suits against Mr. Clay on two occasions."

"Yeah, and as I am sure you know, I was the loser both times. That damn newspaper's lawyers were a vicious bunch. They dug up all sorts of things that had nothing to do with the suits. Those guys must have majored in character assassination back in law school."

"I am not about to defend the legal profession," Wolfe said. "I will leave that to others. It is my understanding that you lavished favors on elected officials in two states, officials who later were forced out of their positions at least in part because of these favors."

"The gifts I gave were well within legal bounds, and I can prove it," Andrews said, coming forward in his chair and poking holes in the air with his index finger. "I was sorry that the election boards in those two states chose to punish these men. They were overly influenced by Clay's spiteful columns."

"Perhaps. I believe at one point you said that Mr. Clay was the 'single worst thing wrong with American journalism today.' Am I accurately quoting you?"

"Sounds like what I said, and I'm not about to retract it."

"Did you ever make threats toward Mr. Clay?"

"Well, I brought those suits against him. But the only times I laid eyes on him were in the courtrooms."

"That was not my question," Wolfe said.

"You mean, did I ever threaten him on the telephone or by mail or telegraph or any other means? The answer is no, and what good would it have done? He apparently decided early on that he did not like me, and nothing I could do would have ever changed that."

"Part of his criticism of you focused on structural problems in buildings you had developed, is that not so?"

Andrews looked down and said nothing for several seconds. When he looked up and faced Wolfe, he shook his head. "I don't know why I should bother explaining this to you, because you obviously are prejudiced against me, as Clay was. But I can only say in my defense that I was lied to on several occasions by contractors who assured me both by their word and by their signed and notarized contracts that they had followed the building and zoning regulations of their respective communities to the letter. The worst violation involved that shopping center in New Jersey, which I assume you are aware of."

"I am," Wolfe said. "That burst water pipe that caused extensive damage to the complex. I seem to recall that you had no comment for Mr. Clay, at least according to his column."

"That's right, and I'll tell you why, dammit. Several years earlier, that bastard called me and wanted a comment about a residential complex I was planning to develop up in Westchester County, near White Plains. I knew very little about Clay at the time. Naively, I figured it would be good public relations for me, given how well read his column was, so I told him all about my plans for these buildings.

"When his column ran the next day, I didn't recognize any of my quotes. He ripped me up one side and down the other, calling me a 'con artist' who wanted to despoil the pristine nature of that part of Westchester with tall buildings, turning the area into what he called 'Manhattan North.' By the way, if you're interested, that column of his killed the project. That was the first and only time I took a telephone call from Cameron Clay."

"You certainly had reason to dislike him."

"That puts me in the company of many other people."

"I will not argue the point," Wolfe said. "Do you know where you were the night, or the early morning, when Mr. Clay died?"

"Refresh me on the date," he said. I gave it to him.

"I was probably at home," Andrews said. "I've got a penthouse place on the Upper West Side. Before you ask, I live alone, and I almost always sleep alone. I have been divorced twice, and I am not about to try finding Wife Number Three."

"Mr. Clay had a similar lack of marital success," Wolfe said.

Andrews ran a hand through his thick hair. "I hope that is the only thing we had in common," he said. "I would not want to find myself associated with the man in any way. If that makes me a suspect in what you believe was his murder, so be it."

"As I indicated to you earlier, I am not yet prepared to state that Mr. Clay was murdered."

"Nice to know you're keeping an open mind," Andrews said after I had refreshed his drink. "At the risk of reversing our roles and making me the interrogator, what did you personally think of Cameron Clay?"

If Wolfe was surprised by the question, he did not show it. "I met the man once and found him to be most unhappy. I would say his was an unfulfilled life."

"If you are trying to generate sympathy for him, you have come to the wrong place," Andrews said.

"Such was not my intention, sir. You chose to ask me a question, and I responded candidly."

"Point taken," Andrews said. "I believe I now have indulged you and Goodwin sufficiently. Do you have any further questions for me?"

"I think not. Mr. Goodwin will see you out."

"Not terribly cordial, was he?" I said to Wolfe when I had returned to the office. "I asked if I could help him flag a taxi, and he said, 'The last thing I need is any help from you.'"

"Perhaps he remains upset at the way you got him to come here."

"We've been over that, and I'm not about to revisit it," I replied. "You wanted to see him, I delivered him. Andrews's only bruises are to his oversize ego, and that can stand a little bruising anyway. Where do we go from here?"

"I would like to know if Mr. Clay made a will, and if so, who its beneficiaries are. Mr. Cohen may be able to give us that information."

"Do you want me to call him now?"

"No, tomorrow will be soon enough."

CHAPTER 25

I called Lon after breakfast. "How nice to hear from you," he said with only the slightest touch of sarcasm in his voice. "Do you have anything to report that I can take to my bosses? Mr. Haverhill, in particular, is getting antsy. And when he gets antsy, we all get antsy."

"Patience, patience. When a master is at work, he must not be hurried."

"Swell. If I tell that to the man who owns the operation, he'll toss me out of his office on the seat of my pants."

"Well, word it another way to him, then. Now, I have a question for you."

"I will try to suppress my shock."

"Do you know if Cameron Clay made a will, and if so, who is the executor?"

"That is actually two questions. But I do happen to have the answers to both. There is a will, and Larry McNeil is its executor. I also have another piece of information that you may find of interest."

"Fire away."

"A modest funeral service is being held for Cameron Clay this very afternoon at a mortuary on the Upper West Side. I will be attending it as the *Gazette*'s representative."

"I am interested; give me the time and place, and there's a good chance I'll show up there myself."

When Wolfe came down from his morning orchid session, I gave him what I knew about Clay's will, and I also suggested that I go to the service in honor of the columnist.

"Do so," he said. "Surely, Mr. McNeil also will be present, and it is likely you can learn more about Mr. Clay's testament from him."

Just before two o'clock, I stepped out of a taxi in front of a two-story brick-and-stone mortuary in the West Seventies between Amsterdam and Columbus Avenues. A handful of other people were just entering, among them Lon Cohen.

"Somehow, I suspected I'd see you," he said. "It's going to be a small gathering. He did not have any relatives to speak of, at least none who lived around here."

We went through the carpeted lobby and were directed by a man in a dark suit into what looked like a small chapel with a few rows of folding chairs facing a lectern up in front. The casket, also at the front, was closed, and there were several flower arrangements grouped around it. By far the largest, supported by a trestle, read IN MEMORY FROM YOUR FRIENDS AND COWORKERS AT THE NEW YORK GAZETTE.

What struck me the most were the four people, two men and two women, who were getting settled in the front row. They all wore the dark uniforms and hats of the Salvation

Army. "What's that all about?" I whispered to Lon as we took seats in the back.

"Beats me. As far as I can recall, Cameron never mentioned the Salvation Army in his columns. Maybe McNeil can enlighten us," he said as Clay's young assistant entered, nodded in our direction, and took a chair across the aisle. I did not recognize anyone else among the seventeen people scattered in the seats ahead of us, some in pairs, others alone.

Piped-in organ music began playing hymns I vaguely recognized from my Sunday school days back in Ohio as we waited. After several minutes, the music faded and a thin, somber young man in a business suit stepped to the lectern and cleared his throat.

"Good afternoon," he intoned somberly, "I am Reverend Marcus Dettmer. Thank you all so much for coming today. We are here to celebrate the life of Cameron Clay, a man known to many thousands through his well-read column in the *New York Gazette*. I never had the privilege of meeting Mr. Clay, but I have learned much about the man from his coworkers on the newspaper, two of whom are here with us today." He nodded toward Lon and Larry McNeil.

Reverend Dettmer cleared his throat again and held the lectern with both hands. "Mr. Clay was born in Maryland, the son of a steelworker and a seamstress, and from his earliest days, he knew that he wanted to be a writer. He attended the University of Maryland, where he studied journalism, and then entered the newspaper business." The young minister droned on, listing the various stops along the way in Clay's career, most of which I tuned out.

But when he got to the present, I began paying attention again. "Cameron Clay was always a fighter for the little guy and against what he felt were the entrenched interests," he said. "To quote an oft-used phrase, but one I believe to be so very relevant in his life, Mr. Clay 'comforted the afflicted and afflicted the comfortable.' It was clear that he struck a chord with readers, as I am told his column was consistently the most popular feature in the *Gazette.* His voice will be missed, and all those who cared for Mr. Clay shall miss him."

The rest of the brief service consisted of a prayer, Bible reading, and the singing of a hymn, "A Mighty Fortress Is Our God." As we filed out of the chapel, I went over to Larry McNeil on the sidewalk. "Can I talk to you for a few minutes?" I asked.

"Sure, Mr. Goodwin. Anything you want."

"First, how did those Salvation Army people happen to be there?"

"Cameron was a great believer in the Salvation Army," he said. "In fact, he left the bulk of his money to them."

"He didn't strike me as the religious type."

"He wasn't, not at all. He used to refer to himself as 'a practicing agnostic.' But the Salvation Army was something different."

"How so?"

"Cameron had no brothers or sisters, only an uncle he was very close to. But this uncle struggled all his adult life. He drank heavily, which cost him his marriage, and he eventually ended up living in flophouses and then on the streets in Baltimore. At the low point in his life, he was living under a railroad viaduct, wrapped in pieces of cardboard. Somehow, a member of the Salvation Army found him there and brought him to their center. They dried him out, worked with him for months, and eventually helped get him a job. He and Cameron got reunited a few months before the old man's death, also thanks to the Salvation Army, and Cameron never forgot it."

"I'll be damned. By the way, did you happen to—"

"Sorry to break in," an elderly man in a threadbare suit said to us, "but do either of you happen to be with the *Gazette*?"

"I am," McNeil said, "why?"

"I've been reading Cameron Clay's column for years," he said, "and it was always the best darned thing in your whole paper."

"Thank you very much, sir," McNeil said. "Do you live nearby?"

"Oh no, I'm from over in New Jersey, Hoboken. But I decided when I saw the notice of this funeral service that I thought I'd pay my respects. I wish I'd known Clay. He was a fighter, like that pastor said. Your paper has lost a good man."

McNeil thanked him, and he shambled off. "Before he came up to us, I was about to ask if you recognized any of the other mourners," I said.

"Not a one," he said. "I guess they must have been readers of the column, like that old guy. I wish more people had shown up, though."

"You said Clay left most of his money to the Salvation Army, and I understand you are the executor."

"I am. Yes, he gave the Salvation Army four hundred thousand dollars plus whatever proceeds come from the sale of his brownstone. I get five grand, partly in thanks for my role as executor, and he made a few small bequests, to his cleaning woman, a tipster he used for column items, and the cabbie who picked him up at home every morning and took him to the office, then drove him back home. Excuse me, Mr. Goodwin, but I need to go back in and talk to the funeral director about his expenses. Another role for an executor."

I thanked McNeil for the information and turned to Lon Cohen, who had been talking to another of the mourners, a woman. "She was telling me how much she liked Stop the

Presses!" he said. "Told me she loved it when he 'stuck it to some big shot,' those were her words. What do you say we share a cab back south?"

Once we were in the yellow cab, Lon turned to me and asked, "Anything strike you about the service?"

"It was pretty plain, and there wasn't much of a turnout."

"Exactly! As I looked around the chapel, I couldn't help thinking that, here was a guy whose name had been known all over town for years. Loved by some, hated by some, read by tens of thousands, maybe more. There were billboards all over town with his picture on them, radio commercials promoting his column. Hell, some people could name him faster than they could tell you who the current mayor is. Yet he dies and less than twenty-five people in all show up to send him off. What does that tell you?"

"First, that Clay didn't have many friends, real friends, maybe by choice. Second, no matter how well known a person seems to be, in most cases he gets forgotten quickly."

"Fame is fleeting, isn't it?" Lon said.

"It sure is. Can you name the last four senators from New York, not counting the current ones?"

"I'd have to think about it for a while."

"Me, too. Does the *Gazette* have plans to replace Clay?"

"I know the brass are in the process of mulling it over. McNeil would seem to be a strong possibility, but I get the impression that Cordwell feels he needs more seasoning."

"Well, he is pretty young all right, but from what Clay had said when we talked to him, he relied on McNeil and thought he would be an able successor."

"Yeah, Cameron had told me that, too, more than once," Lon said. "'I've trained that kid well,' he liked to say. He was proud of Larry."

"Here we are at the brownstone," I said, pulling out my bill-fold as I climbed out of the car.

"Put your money away," Lon said. "This one's on the *Gazette*. I'll take your dough next time we sit down at Saul's poker table."

I started to give him a retort, but the cab already had begun to pull away, bound for the offices of America's fifth-largest newspaper.

CHAPTER 26

When Wolfe came down from the plant rooms, he first asked me about Clay's will, and I told him of the Salvation Army bequest.

"A noble organization," he said. "However, I would not have expected Mr. Clay to be a supporter of theirs, despite what they did to aid his uncle."

"That surprised me as well. Maybe there was someone with an honest-to-goodness heart under that hard-shell exterior."

"Perhaps. Tell me about the funeral service."

I gave him one of my verbatim reports. One of my strengths has always been the ability to recite back conversations and other events word-for-word. Because of the brevity of Clay's service, this was hardly a challenge.

As I did the recitation, Wolfe leaned back in his chair, hands interlaced over his belly. After finishing, I got no reaction and started to ask him what he thought, but I caught myself. His eyes were closed and lips were pushing in and out, in and out. Even if I had spoken, he would not have heard me. He was somewhere else and I couldn't reach him. No one could when he was in this state.

Excited as I was, there was nothing for me to do but wait. I timed him, as I always did when he was in one of these trances. Fritz stepped into the office to say something, probably a question for Wolfe about dinner, but I put a finger to my lips and pointed at the man in the chair. Fritz understood immediately and backed out without a sound. He's seen this exercise many times, and his face registered excitement.

Thirty-eight minutes later, Wolfe opened his eyes wide and came forward in his chair, resting his hands palms down on his desk blotter. "Archie, there are times when I ignore the obvious, as I have done here. I sit before you chagrined."

I had no idea what he was talking about, so I kept quiet.

"I need to see them all," he said.

"By all of them, you mean . . . ?"

"Everyone: Mr. Cohen and his superiors at the *Gazette*, the five individuals whom Mr. Clay feared, and Mr. McNeil."

"I don't like to be a naysayer, but that may be difficult. It was hard enough to get those five potential murderers here once, with the exception of Serena Sanchez, who came willingly, and it will be even harder to bring them back without having them delivered here bound and gagged."

"If this makes things easier for you, tell them I now know how Mr. Clay died, and it will be in their best interest to attend a meeting here."

"Are you planning to invite Inspector Cramer as well?"

"I am, which probably means that if he comes, and I believe he will, he will bring our old friend Sergeant Stebbins along with him."

"Old friend indeed. Should I tell our guests the police will be represented?"

"No, let it be a surprise," Wolfe said. Because of his trance, he had not rung for beer, which he did now. When Fritz brought in two chilled bottles and a glass on a tray, he wore a puzzled expression. I winked at him and silently mouthed the words, *I'll fill you in later.*

As usual, I was several miles behind Wolfe, although I was beginning to get a glimmer, albeit a faint one. "When do you want to have this gathering?" I asked Wolfe.

"Would I be unreasonable to suggest tomorrow night?" he said.

Well, here we go again, I said to myself. "Of course you would, but what's new about that?" I warned Wolfe that it might be several days before I could get these people rounded up, but he held fast. Where to start? For no particular reason, I chose Councilman Millard Beardsley and dialed his office on 125th Street.

The same silken-voiced young woman I had talked to on the phone before answered.

"Is this April?" I asked, recalling her name from my visit to Beardsley's office.

"Yes, it is. How may I help you, sir?"

"My name is Goodwin, Archie Goodwin. You may remember me from my visit a few days ago."

"Yes, yes, I do, Mr. Goodwin," April said, caution entering into her tone. She obviously had not forgotten my scuffle with the slow-moving bodyguard. "How may I help you, Mr. Goodwin?"

"I would like to talk to Mr. Beardsley. Is he in the office today?"

"No, he is out in the district, visiting constituents. May I have him telephone you?"

I gave her our number and said it was extremely important that I talk to him as soon as possible. "I will give him your message, sir, as soon as he returns, which I expect will be within the next hour." I wanted to prolong the conversation, just to hear her voice, but I merely thanked her.

Not twenty minutes later, the phone rang. "Really, Mr. Goodwin," Millard Beardsley said, "I felt we had finished transacting our business when I visited you and Mr. Wolfe. What is it this time?"

"Mr. Wolfe has completed his investigation into the death of Cameron Clay's death, and he wishes to see you and several other individuals to discuss the matter."

"To 'discuss the matter,' you say? Precisely what does that mean? And who are these other individuals?"

"Let me counter your questions with a question of my own. Do you have anything to fear by being present at this gathering?"

"I do not!"

"I can only tell you that all the others who will be here are Caucasian. Perhaps that is a stumbling block for you."

"I beg your pardon, Mr. Goodwin," Beardsley snapped. "That could be construed as a racist remark."

"I assure you, it was not meant as one. I merely felt I should give you some idea of the audience."

"You would give me a better idea if you gave me their names."

"I cannot do that, but I will say that you will know who several of them are."

"For some reason I am unable to pinpoint, I find you engaging, Mr. Goodwin. Although to be candid, I am not entirely sure I can trust you—or your very wily and intelligent employer, for that matter."

"*Wily*? I like that word. Maybe I'll throw it at him the next time we have an argument. And we have our share of them. I don't know what I can do to make you trust me, Mr. Beardsley, except to say this: What is the worst thing that can happen to you if you attend this gathering? I have gotten the impression—correct me if I am wrong—that you are secure in your position as a spokesman for some of this city's most downtrodden and underprivileged residents. Is that a fair statement?"

I waited several seconds for a response. "You are wily yourself, Mr. Goodwin," he said. "You are good-looking, smart, and well spoken. Have you ever considered running for public office?"

"Heaven forbid! I would not wish such an eventuality upon the citizens of New York. Of course, I could never get elected to anything, including dogcatcher, not that I would want to. This city is in enough trouble as it is. It needs more people like you, who are able to express concern for those who for many reasons suffer."

I could hear Beardsley exhaling. "When does Mr. Wolfe want to see me?"

"Tomorrow night, nine o'clock."

"I am placing a certain amount of trust in you, Mr. Goodwin, for good or ill. If I attend this . . . this *performance*, I don't know what else to call it, will I be held up to ridicule?"

"I cannot conceive of any situation in which you would be the subject of ridicule," I told him, secure in the honesty of my response.

"Very well," Beardsley said in a voice barely above a whisper. "I will be there at nine. I do know the way."

I cradled the phone, wondering how all of this would play out. I had been with Wolfe for so long that I had almost absolute trust in his ability to pull a rabbit out of a hat. But I felt that on this case, we were in uncharted waters, and I had an uneasiness as to the result.

However, I was not being paid to fret and anguish, nor were those emotions I indulged in, so I pressed on.

CHAPTER 27

My next call was to Michael Tobin, one-time scourge of the New York City Police Department. I did not have his home number in Yonkers but gambled that he'd be at the florist where he worked part-time and where I had met him. I won the gamble.

"Osborne's Florist, the oldest and best in all of Yonkers, how may I help you?" came the sandpapery voice of the former cop.

"Yes, you can be of help, Mr. Tobin," I said. "You may remember me, Archie Goodwin, from Nero Wolfe's office."

"I remember you. How could I forget? What's the play?"

"The play is that Mr. Wolfe is hosting a gathering tomorrow night in which he will reveal who killed Cameron Clay."

"Why should that affect me?" he snarled. "I had nothing to do with it."

"Then you have nothing to fear, either, do you? It certainly would look odd if you were to be the only one of the five apparent suspects to stay away."

"Since when am I even a suspect?"

"I said *apparent* suspect."

"All right, wise guy, just what's in it for me if I show up—again—at Wolfe's place? Tell me that, will ya?"

"It will show that you're confident enough of your innocence to make an appearance."

"Are any cops going to be there?"

"That I don't know. Mr. Wolfe doesn't always take me into his confidence. I'm just a gofer."

"Is that so? Sorry, but I don't buy it. You seemed to me to be right at home in that nice layout of Wolfe's, almost like you owned the joint yourself."

"I put on a good act. He puts up with me only partly because I know how to mix a good drink for his guests."

"Well, those martinis you gave me were the real thing, I'll give you that much, Goodwin. If I come to this party of yours, will I know any of the others?"

"I can't say for sure, because I don't know who you know. What have you got to lose by showing up? I promise to mix you another martini, or maybe even two."

"I don't like the setup. I didn't kill Clay, although I didn't do any crying when I heard he was dead. But if the cops need a fall guy, hell, I'm made to order for them. The top guys, particularly Humbert, are still sore that I got what they felt was a light sentence. They'd love to see me get life for this, or better yet, fry in that funny-looking throne with wires attached that they have up at Sing-Sing."

"What have you got to lose? You say you're clean on the Clay business. Can anyone prove you were at his place when he caught it?"

"Hell, you already know I don't have an alibi for that night, and I've got a record. That's all DA's hotshots need."

"Maybe Wolfe will pin the tail on another donkey tomorrow night."

"Maybe, but I don't like my chances."

"If that's the case, what's the difference whether you stay home or show up at West Thirty-Fifth Street? At least if you're with us, you can defend yourself."

"Not that it would do a damned bit of good. But what the hell, you're right. I might as well show up. If your boss is going to hand me to the cops, I'll at least go down fighting. I feel like I'm boxed in."

"It's possible you may be, but whatever happens, I've always heard that you're one tough, hard-nosed son of a gun."

"You're goddamn right about that, Goodwin. Okay, I will show up at your place, and I'll also take you up on one or maybe two of those martinis of yours. They may be the last ones I'll ever have."

Next up, I decided, was Roswell Stokes, aka "The Vulture." Rather than trying to beard the man in his favorite restaurant, I chose the frontal attack, calling him at his law firm, the prestigious Mason, Chalmers, and Stokes.

"Mr. Stokes is in conference at the moment, sir," a crisp female voice recited. I say *recited* because it was surely her standard reply to anyone who called him out of the blue.

"Well, if you would be so kind as to tell him Archie Goodwin telephoned, and it is important that I speak to him as soon as possible. He will understand the urgency," I added, giving her our number.

Ten minutes later, I heard from the attorney. "All right, what do you want this time, Goodwin?" he demanded.

"First off, I didn't want you to think I only use sixth-grade stunts in my work. Sometimes I take a more direct approach, which I'm doing now. Second, Nero Wolfe has come to a conclusion about the death of Cameron Clay."

"Am I supposed to start cheering at this point?"

"I don't care how you choose to react, Mr. Stokes. But my boss is hosting a gathering tomorrow night of all the interested parties."

"I repeat my earlier comment. Should I cheer and applaud?"

"You should show up at the brownstone tomorrow night at nine."

"What if I stay away?"

"Your absence will be duly noted."

"By whom?"

"I will leave that to your imagination, sir."

"I have heard, and read, about these 'I will now name the culprit' circuses that Nero Wolfe likes to hold. I've never understood how he—or you—gets all the suspects to show up for his performances, not that I am a suspect in this situation, mind you."

"Well, since you say you are not a suspect, why not come anyway and consider yourself an interested onlooker? As one who specializes in confrontation and persuasion, you'd find Mr. Wolfe's methods intriguing and maybe even enlightening, I would think."

"I don't need to be enlightened by Nero Wolfe."

"Have it your way, but you would be missing a most interesting evening."

"Who all will be there?" Stokes asked. "All of those people who Clay claimed to be of the most danger to him?"

"Yes, that's right, assuming you are not the lone absentee."

"Who else?"

"That I am not at liberty to say. I can tell you, however, that no one in attendance should come as a surprise to you."

"You're pretty damned coy, aren't you?"

"I've never thought of it that way. I simply follow orders, which I find is the best way to conduct myself."

A long pause followed before Stokes broke the silence. "For some strange reason, Goodwin, and don't ask me to explain it, I've decided to accept your offer. I don't know if Nero Wolfe has ever been tripped up before, but I believe he will be this time, and I want to be there to see it."

"Who knows, you may very well be right," I told him. "If so, it will be an event well worth witnessing."

CHAPTER 28

I cradled the receiver and leaned back, stretching. Three down and three to go, counting Larry McNeil. I was getting damned tired of cajoling people into coming to the brownstone. *Wolfe doesn't pay me enough for this kind of work*, I thought. *Already on this case, I've told so many lies I've lost count of them, to say nothing of the half-truths and deceptions I have been a party to.*

Next, I decided to tackle Serena Sanchez, so to speak. My watch read six thirty, which meant she might be back in her hotel room after a session at the Juilliard. My luck held, and she answered on the third ring.

"Archie Goodwin," she said with a lilt. "It is nice to hear your voice."

"The feeling is mutual. I am calling with an invitation to visit Mr. Wolfe again."

"Why is that? I thought everything got covered when I was there before."

"This meeting is a little different. Mr. Wolfe has come to a conclusion as to how your ex-husband died, and he wants to explain it to all those who have an interest in the case."

"And what is that conclusion?"

"I don't know, because he hasn't shared it with me."

"I find that difficult to believe," Serena said.

"You must keep in mind that Mr. Wolfe is a genius, while I am not and never will be. I can make a guess as to what he has concluded, but that is all it would be, a guess."

"Will you share that guess with me?"

"No, because I don't want to appear foolish if I am totally off the target, which is likely."

"You would never appear foolish to me, Archie."

"Thank you for that. But I'm going to keep my thoughts to myself for now. I am hoping you will come to the brownstone tomorrow night at nine."

"I had a dinner engagement, but I believe I can change it if you think it's important that I be there."

"It is most important, Serena."

"Very well, I will come, Archie. But don't worry about getting a taxi for me this time. I can do that myself."

"Too bad. I'm sure Mr. Aronson would have liked to hear more of your opera stories."

She laughed. "I am afraid I told him every single story I have. I would be repeating myself. But he was very nice to be so interested."

"It was genuine. I will see you tomorrow night."

My next call was to Kerwin Andrews. I had his office number and dialed it, getting no answer, which was hardly surprising given the time. Then I tried Larry McNeil's home number, again striking out.

I turned to Wolfe, who was doing a *New York Times* crossword puzzle. "Here's a progress report," I said. "Tobin, Beardsley, Stokes, and Miss Sanchez have promised to be here tomorrow night. Not surprising, nobody was very happy about being summoned once again, least of all Tobin and Stokes. I will try Andrews and McNeil in the morning. Any other instructions?"

"No. I will call Inspector Cramer in the morning. He, too, will not be happy to be invited."

"But I've got a crisp Hamilton in my pocket that says he will show up."

"No bet. The inspector is highly predictable. He will be here, as will his sergeant."

The next morning after breakfast, I tried Andrews again at his office, this time with success, as a secretary put me through to him.

"I thought we said all we needed to when I was at your place," he said in a surly tone. "What's this all about?"

"Nero Wolfe has an announcement to make about the death of Cameron Clay, and he felt you would want to be present to hear it."

"What on earth for? Wolfe has a direct line to the *Gazette*, as I understand it. I can just wait and read it in the next day's edition."

"Mr. Wolfe has expressly asked that you be part of the gathering tomorrow night at nine."

"Why?"

"I am not privy to the reasons, but his are always sound ones."

"Give me the guest list."

"The four others besides you who Mr. Clay suspected of being behind the threatening telephone calls he received."

"That's all?"

"That's all I am aware of," I lied . . . yet again.

"Why do I feel like I'd be walking into a trap if I showed up at Wolfe's little party?"

"Can you give me a good reason why Nero Wolfe would want to trap you?"

"I think the whole thing's a frame-up. Somebody wants to pin Clay's murder on me. If that sounds paranoid, I'm sorry, but that's how I see it."

"If you're talking about the police doing the framing, they really don't want to see the murder pinned on anybody, it doesn't suit their purposes. The murder rate in the city is already way up year over year, and they would far rather see Cameron Clay's death go into the books as a suicide. Surely, you can understand that."

"I still don't know why I have to show up. I humored Wolfe once, and that should be more than enough. Or is some relative of Clay's trying to get revenge on me because I had the nerve to sue him?"

"As far as I'm aware, Mr. Clay has no living relatives, or at least none who are close to him. If an individual wants to 'pin' Clay's murder on you, as you phrase it, that person likely would do so whether you show up here tonight or not. Wouldn't it be better for you to be present so you can defend yourself against any charges that might arise?"

"Hah, so somebody will be there accusing me."

"I did not say that, Mr. Andrews. To my knowledge, no one will level charges against you, but in the unlikely occurrence that such is the case, you would be far better served by being present."

"You've got an answer for everything, don't you?" he said petulantly.

"Only an answer for every objection you have thus far

raised. Believe me, sir, tonight's gathering is not intended as a 'Get Kerwin Andrews' feeding frenzy."

He exhaled loudly. "Can you give me any guarantees?"

"Only that you will be treated fairly."

"*Fairly* is a relative term, Mr. Goodwin. What seems fair to you may well seem unjust to me."

"I can only say you will not be railroaded. Beyond that, I can say no more, except to point out that you would be most conspicuous by your absence."

"Well, I certainly would not want to be conspicuous, would I? So if I came to Wolfe's place, it will be at my peril?"

"I would rather say that it will be to your advantage."

"We seem to be talking past each other," he said. "All right, I will be there. Can I bring my attorney?"

"No, you cannot. No one else who is coming tonight will have legal counsel accompanying them."

"It seems I just can't buy a break with you, can I? Okay, have it your way. I will see you at nine, prepared for some dirty tricks."

"There will be no dirty tricks, I promise you that, Mr. Andrews." He mumbled something unintelligible and hung up.

I was definitely going to ask Wolfe for a raise. He may have the brains on our team—no argument there—but I have the finesse. There is no way in the world that he could have sweet-talked this motley bunch into coming to the brownstone not once but twice in the last several days. I was worn out from cajoling and figurative arm-twisting, and I felt like a drink. But that was not about to happen this early in the day—I rarely drink in daylight, and almost never in the winter. Besides, I still had one call to make: To Larry McNeil, Clay's loyal assistant.

I tried him at the *Gazette*, with success. "Are you still going through Clay's files?" I asked.

"Yes, sir, I am. It seems he never threw anything away, which doesn't surprise me given his pack-rat mentality. Most of what we've found is old reporters' notebooks full of unintelligible—at least to me—scribblings, as well as letters to readers dating back years, some of them polite, some rude, depending on the tone of the letters he received from them."

"So it's a walk, of sorts, down memory lane. It brings back memories for you, I'm sure. I'm calling to invite you to Nero Wolfe's residence tonight at nine. He plans to announce his findings regarding Mr. Clay's death, and he knew you would want to be present."

"Really? What has he come up with, Mr. Goodwin?"

"I don't know. He has not chosen to share his findings with me, which is not without precedent."

"Will . . . those five be there?"

"You mean the ones he suspected as the likeliest to be behind the telephone calls? Yes, they will."

"One of them has to be guilty," McNeil said with fervor. "I'm dying to know who it is."

"You will not have to wait long to find out."

"That is a great relief to me, Mr. Goodwin," McNeil said. "Part of the reason I insisted on going through all of Cameron's papers is that I hoped to find something, anything at all, that might point to who killed him."

"Has anything helpful turned up?"

"No, nothing whatever. I'm not surprised, but I really had hoped I might somehow get lucky and find a clue of some sort. Can you give me any idea of what to expect tonight?"

"I really can't, because I don't know myself. Mr. Wolfe does not always share his plans with yours truly, as I alluded to a few minutes ago."

"Other than me, will anyone from the *Gazette* be there tonight?"

"That much I can tell you, as they are Mr. Wolfe's clients in this investigation. I believe you may see both the owner and the editor." I did not mention Lon Cohen, as I wasn't sure Wolfe planned to invite him.

"I will be there tonight, Mr. Goodwin. I'm looking forward to it."

So was I, although likely for different reasons.

CHAPTER 29

Wolfe came down from the plant rooms, placed orchids in his desk vase, and rang for beer. After asking if I had slept well, he riffled through the morning mail.

"All of the people you requested be present tonight have answered in the affirmative," I told him.

"Satisfactory. Get Mr. Cohen on the telephone."

Still recovering from getting two "satisfactory" comments on the same case—a first—I dialed Lon's number as Wolfe picked up his instrument.

"Mr. Cohen, this is Nero Wolfe, with Archie also on the line. I am prepared to announce my findings regarding Mr. Clay's death. Can you arrange to have Mr. Haverhill and Mr. Cordwell present at nine tonight?"

"I don't know what other plans they might have made, but I have a feeling they would quickly cancel them in light of your meeting."

"I would also like you to be present, if it does not inconvenience you."

"I wouldn't miss it. I will call both of them and get back to Archie."

After we hung up, Wolfe took a sip of beer and dabbed his lips with a handkerchief. "Now call Inspector Cramer," he said, again picking up his receiver.

"Good morning, Inspector, it's Archie Goodwin. Mr. Wolfe would like to speak to you."

"Yeah, well I'd like to talk to him, too," he muttered.

"I am on the line," Wolfe said.

"Well, it's your nickel," Cramer said. "You go first."

"Very well. I have come to a conclusion regarding the death of Cameron Clay, and I plan to discuss that conclusion here tonight at nine."

"Another one of your shows, huh? And I assume you plan to prove it was murder, not suicide."

"That can wait until tonight. I thought you might want to be present."

"Damned right I want to be present, and I'll bring Stebbins with me."

"I assumed you would, and he will be welcome. Now you had a subject you wanted to discuss with me."

"You've already covered it. I wanted to know what progress you had made, if any, on the Clay business, and I gather that I will find out tonight."

"You will, sir."

"But I do have a question at that. Are you planning to publicly embarrass the police department tonight, and by extension, me?"

"I am not, sir, you have my word on that." That drew a snort from the inspector, who banged down his telephone.

The phone rang seconds later. "My bosses both will be there tonight," Lon Cohen said. "But Eric Haverhill demands to know what you have found out."

"He will learn that tonight, Mr. Cohen."

"It doesn't seem like he can wait that long. He's going to be calling you. I tried to put him off, but he can be the proverbial bull in the china shop. Cordwell also tried to put the brakes on him without success. Be prepared for a call—very soon."

"Very soon" came not a half minute after Lon hung up. "This is Eric Haverhill. I would like to speak to Mr. Wolfe," he said curtly.

I cupped the speaker and whispered Haverhill's name to Wolfe, who scowled and picked up his phone.

"This is Nero Wolfe."

"Eric Haverhill here. I understand you are going to name Cameron Clay's killer tonight."

"I am going to summarize my findings," Wolfe corrected. "I trust you will be present."

"This comes with no advance notice whatever. I am an extremely busy man, as I know you can appreciate."

"I do appreciate that, sir, and I apologize for the late notice, but it could not be helped."

"Huh! Well, I have changed some plans to suit you, so I will be able to be there. But I need to know in advance who you have identified as Clay's killer."

"I'm sorry, Mr. Haverhill, but it doesn't work that way. You and everyone else who will be present tonight will learn of my findings together."

"But I am your client, dammit!"

"You are indeed, sir. That entitles you to a full explanation of what I have determined, and you will receive that explanation tonight, not before."

"I've got to tell my wife something. She's dying to know who killed Clay."

"Feel free to bring her with you tonight then."

"Oh no, she would be uncomfortable in that gathering. I assume all of the suspects will be present."

"They will."

"And will members of the police be there as well?"

"Yes."

"What about Commissioner Humbert?"

"He has not been invited. It would surprise me were he to appear."

"Well, that's something anyway. I don't think I could stand to look at him again. The man is an incompetent. There is no other way to describe him."

"I will see you here at nine o'clock, sir," Wolfe said, hanging up on his client.

"That's one way to shut him up," I said. "I just hope he doesn't fire you after all we've been through."

"Mr. Haverhill is impulsive and impatient. I am sure he poses challenges for Mr. Cordwell as he tries to edit and publish his newspaper."

"No doubt. Haverhill seems to be a loose cannon."

"Another one of your colorful phrasings. There are times when I feel I need a translator when talking to you," Wolfe said.

"I have felt the same way about your vocabulary for years," I replied. "At last things are beginning to even up between us."

That afternoon, while Wolfe was upstairs with his orchids, I got the office ready for the evening's festivities. We would have eleven guests, counting Cramer and Stebbins, who usually chose to stand in the back of the room. So that meant we needed seating for nine, including the red leather chair, where

Haverhill, as the client, would be parked. I lined up two rows of chairs, four in each row, in front of the desk.

Then I stocked the bar, taking our guests' preferences into consideration. I made sure there was plenty of scotch for Haverhill, Cordwell, Andrews, and Lon Cohen; a bottle of the single-malt scotch for Millard Beardsley; rye for Roswell Stokes; martini mixings for Tobin; and sherry for Serena Sanchez.

As I was puttering in the office, Fritz stood in the doorway with an anxious expression. "We are having guests tonight, Archie?"

"We sure are. Mr. Wolfe is going to put on one of his shows, which will mean more money in the bank."

"I hope he is getting enough to eat," he said, wringing his hands. Fritz worries when Wolfe has to go to work, and he worries when we don't have a case. There's no pleasing the man.

"I wouldn't fret about his food intake. You of all people know how much he's getting, and it's more than what two average humans combined consume."

He nodded, but the concerned look stayed on his puss as he returned to the kitchen to put the finishing touches on tonight's dinner, *cassoulet de Castelnaudry*, which I refer to as "boiled beans," much to Fritz's dismay. They were my favorite beans, however, and as was often the case when this was the main course, it would be followed by pumpkin pie.

As invariably happens when Wolfe holds one of his revelations, he was calm and relaxed in the hours leading up to the night's events, while I got the jitters. Part of the reason for this tendency may be that he knows precisely where he's going, while I am usually in the dark, at least to some degree. At dinner, he held forth on how and why the population growth of the United States was continuing to shift to the South and the West.

"Does that mean we should move to Los Angeles or Miami to be part of the trend?" I said, to which he shuddered.

Wolfe not only would never live anywhere but in New York City, he also considers trips to such far-flung places like Philadelphia or Boston as major expeditions to be avoided at all costs. Sure, he has left the brownstone—and the city—on rare occasions, but only for what he considers extremely good reasons.

After dinner, he returned to the office with his coffee to read, while I puttered at my desk, rearranging drawers that didn't need rearranging, then went to the safe to count the petty cash, which added up, and to oil my pistols. I consulted my watch every ten minutes, then went to the kitchen to see if Fritz needed any help—he didn't—and I realized that my presence there was making him nervous as well.

Finally, I put my overcoat and hat on and walked around the block to kill time. It was a clear, crisp night, with a sky full of stars and a crescent moon. I drew in the February air, finding that it and the walk calmed me, and I returned to the brownstone at twenty-five minutes to nine, ready for the show to begin.

CHAPTER 30

When the doorbell rang at five minutes to nine, I was correct in assuming it was Inspector Cramer, who always shows up first for these shindigs of Wolfe's. Also as usual, he was accompanied by Sergeant Purley Stebbins, with whom I have had a mutual dislike for years.

"Welcome," I said to Cramer, who looked mad enough to chew on a chair leg. If he held true to form, he would get progressively angrier as the evening went on.

He mumbled something unintelligible in reply to my greeting and bulled his way in, hanging up his hat and coat. I merely nodded to Stebbins, with whom I rarely share words. He screwed up his bony, square-jawed face and did not even bother to return my nod. That pretty much summarizes the way it is with the two of us.

I followed the two cops into the office, where they took their usual places, standing, backs against the wall, behind the rows of chairs. "Wolfe's waiting in the wings so he can make his typical entrance," Cramer observed, jamming an unlit stogie into his mouth.

"It's comforting that you know the drill after all these years," I told the inspector, then, upon hearing the bell, headed back down the hall to answer the door. It was the *Gazette* trio, with Eric Haverhill casting himself as the mopey-looking member of the group. I let them in, and the paper's owner pushed past me as if I were invisible. Like Cramer, he chose to hang up his own coat, while I did the honors for Cordwell and Lon, both of whom thanked me.

I directed them all to the office, not that they needed any directing. Haverhill went straight for the red leather chair, thereby eliminating part of my role as usher. As he sat, the *Gazette*'s owner turned toward Cramer and Stebbins, his face reflecting a momentary puzzlement. Then he nodded his understanding and allowed himself a tight smile.

"Hello, Mr. Cramer, glad to see you. I guess you won't be leaving here tonight empty-handed, will you?"

Cramer said nothing as I gestured Cordwell and Lon to seats in the front row. The bell squawked again, and I was off to the door, opening it to the grim-faced expressions of Tobin and Andrews, who did not appear to know each other. I went through the coat routine with them and got them seated in the last two front row seats, then headed back to the door.

The last four guests had arrived simultaneously, and I breathed a sigh; everybody had showed. The three men, Stokes, Beardsley, and McNeil, deferred to Serena Sanchez, who entered first and gave me one of her high-wattage smiles.

"See, I am here and I am on time, Archie Goodwin," she purred. "I'll bet you thought I was going to be late. I have a reputation for that, but not tonight."

"I never doubted you would be prompt," I said, smiling back and hanging up her sable as the others took off their own coats. After leading them to the office, I directed Serena to the chair in the back row that was farthest from my desk, put Beardsley next to her, then Stokes, and on my end, Larry McNeil.

"Somebody's missing," Stokes snorted.

"Mr. Wolfe will be with us shortly," I told him, going behind his desk and pressing the buzzer. Thirty seconds later, he entered the office and circled behind his desk, sitting. He studied the assemblage and nodded. "Thank you all for coming tonight," he said. "Do you know one another, or should I commence with introductions?"

"You can *dispense* with introductions, Wolfe," Stokes said with a sneer, pleased with his play on words. "I believe we all have a pretty good idea who's sitting around us. What we don't know is why in hell we're here."

"I hope that soon will be apparent, Mr. Stokes," Wolfe replied, pressing the same buzzer that I had a minute earlier. "First, I am going to have beer, and Mr. Goodwin will be glad to serve drinks to each of you. Give him your orders."

"I did not realize this was a social occasion," Kerwin Andrews snapped.

"It is not, sir, although I prefer a level of civility that I believe is best maintained in an atmosphere of cordiality, and I believe beverages can help to sustain that atmosphere."

"Well said, Mr. Wolfe, very well said," Millard Beardsley put in, nodding and clapping twice. "I will have your best scotch, as I did on my previous visit."

"And as I recall, you want that straight up, because adding water is a sin," I said. "Do I have that right?"

"You do, Mr. Goodwin, you most surely do," the councilman answered with a grin.

"Mr. Stokes, I believe you prefer rye on the rocks."

"Yes," the lawyer said, "if you please."

"And for you, a martini, I recall," I said to Tobin, who nodded grimly, arms folded over his chest. He had apparently decided he would maintain a surly attitude tonight.

"Miss Sanchez, would you like a sherry?"

"Nothing, Arch—Mr. Goodwin. I seem to have a headache."

"An aspirin, perhaps?"

"No, no, nothing."

"Mr. McNeil, you like beer, and in the bottle. That leaves several other scotch drinkers to be taken care of," I said. "And you take yours with soda," I added for Kerwin Andrews. "You gentlemen of the press, scotch on the rocks for each, I presume." I got agreement all around and delivered the drinks as Wolfe watched with approval. He knew I was putting on a show to ease the tension in the room.

"Now that everyone who wants one has a libation," Wolfe said after everyone was served, "I would—"

"Excuse me, who are they and what are they doing here?" Kerwin Andrews interrupted, gesturing toward Cramer and Stebbins.

"They are Inspector Cramer and Sergeant Stebbins of the New York City Police Department's Homicide Squad, and they are here at my invitation."

"I know who they are," Tobin said, turning around and glowering at the cops and getting glowers in return. "I also know what this is, seeing them here. What we have is a goddamn kangaroo court, and I am being set up for the murder of Cameron Clay."

Before Wolfe could respond, Serena Sanchez cut in. "I am sorry, Mr. Wolfe, but despite what that one gentleman said"—she gestured toward Stokes—"I do not know who any of these people are," she said, looking around, "or even why they—and I—are here tonight."

"My apologies, Miss Sanchez," Wolfe said. "You are correct that I should have made introductions, which I now will do. Eric Haverhill, owner of the *New York Gazette*, occupies the red chair at the end of my desk. In the front row, starting on my left, are Ashton Cordwell, editor of the *Gazette*, and Lon Cohen, also of the *Gazette*. Next are Kerwin Andrews, a well-known real estate developer, and Michael Tobin, late of the New York City Police Department.

"In the back row," Wolfe continued, "City Councilman Millard Beardsley is on your immediate left, and next to him is Roswell Stokes, a prominent defense attorney. On the end sits Larry McNeil, who was an assistant to Mr. Clay at the *Gazette* for the last five years. And the woman who posed the question is Serena Sanchez, an opera singer who once was married to Cameron Clay.

"Now as to the reason for this gathering: I was commissioned by Mr. Haverhill and Mr. Cordwell to investigate the death of Cameron Clay to determine whether he was murdered, and if so, by whom. You call this a kangaroo court, Mr. Tobin. I assure you it is no such thing, and I suggest you withhold judgment until I am finished.

"In the days leading up to his death," Wolfe continued, "Mr. Clay reported that he had received telephone calls threatening his life. He said he felt these calls were instigated by one of five persons, all of whom are in this room: Mr. Andrews, Mr. Tobin, Mr. Beardsley, Mr. Stokes, and Miss Sanchez. And not one of them has a plausible alibi for the overnight period during which Mr. Clay died."

That started a chattering among the guests that Wolfe halted by slapping a palm on his desktop. "If you please, let me continue. All of these five had their reasons for enmity toward Mr. Clay, who had written disparaging things about each of them in his newspaper column."

"Disparaging things, hell! They were more than that, they were downright libelous, at least in my case," Andrews spat.

"Perhaps," Wolfe said, "although I will leave that to the lawyers to determine. Mr. Stokes, as our legal expert, do you feel Cameron Clay made actionable comments in the *Gazette*?"

"I would need to review all of his columns and study his comments case by case, but since I have no interest in reading his amateurish prose, I would not waste my time," the attorney said. "However, some things that he wrote about me—quite a few of them, in fact—definitely were actionable. I chose not to take action, however."

"Mr. Andrews, I know you did file suits against the columnist."

"I did, and as you also well know, I was unsuccessful on two occasions, thanks to the tactics used by the *Gazette*'s lawyers," Andrews said, looking daggers at both Haverhill and Cordwell. "But despite how I felt about Cameron Clay, I was not about to kill him, for heaven's sake."

"Nobody has killed him!" Cramer roared from the back of the room. "The man committed suicide, plain and simple. Let's be clear about that. He shot himself, and I dare anyone to prove that he didn't."

That comment led to another outburst from the assemblage, including some excited and angry comments, with people talking over one another in the clamor. Once again, Wolfe stilled the furor, this time with four words: "Inspector Cramer is correct."

CHAPTER 31

Jaws dropped, eyebrows shot up, Serena gasped, and no words were spoken for close to half a minute. Everyone wore a surprised expression, no one more than Inspector Lionel T. Cramer, although Purley Stebbins was a close second.

The silence was broken by Roswell Stokes. "If what you say is true, why in the name of God are we here?"

"A valid question, sir, and one to which I will respond. I became involved in this affair when Mr. Clay was still alive. He reported to his superiors, and later to me, that he had received a number of hostile telephone calls, some of them strongly suggesting that he was in mortal peril. However, no one else had heard any of these calls. They had only Mr. Clay's word that they had occurred."

"That's not true, Mr. Wolfe," Larry McNeil said after clearing his throat. "He received one of these calls one morning when I was at his home for our daily meetings."

"Did you hear the voice of the person on the other end of the line?" Wolfe asked.

"Well, no. But the telephone did ring, and Cameron seemed very unsettled by the call. I only heard what he said, which was something like 'What the hell do you want?' "

"We will come back to that call later," Wolfe said. "Mr. McNeil, tell us what you found on that fateful day at Cameron Clay's townhouse."

"We've been through all this before," Cramer said, "and the papers have reported it."

"Indulge me please, Mr. Cramer," Wolfe replied, turning toward McNeil.

"I was surprised when I got to Cameron's place, because his front door was ajar, as I have reported before," the young man said, swallowing hard. "I went upstairs to his living room and found him sitting on the sofa. At first, I thought he was dozing, that had happened a few times before, but it didn't take me long to figure out he was dead. There was a hole in his right temple, and he had no pulse. His pistol was on the cushion next to him. After checking his carotid, I telephoned the police, and two officers got there maybe ten minutes later."

"The medical examiner's report indicated that Mr. Clay died between one and four in the morning. Where were you during that time?"

"I've already told you, and the police," McNeil said, turning around and looking at Cramer, who nodded. "I was at a bachelor party at a restaurant in the Village until almost six thirty. After I left there, and not in the best of condition, I'm afraid, I went home to clean up and change before going to see Cameron."

"I understand that several friends who were with you at this bacchanalian revelry confirmed your presence there straight through until the time when the festivities broke up."

"Yes, sir."

"Just so. You also knew that Mr. Clay was terminally ill with cancer and may not have had much more than a year to live."

"I knew that, and later, so did others at the *Gazette*," he said, looking at Haverhill and then at Cordwell and Lon.

"Mr. Clay was a man possessed of intense emotions," Wolfe remarked, "the strongest of which was anger, anger at injustice, at irresponsibility, at graft, at the violation of public trust. However, lest I paint him as a man with only noble intentions, I should point out that often his anger was irrational and petty. He excoriated his ex-wife"—Wolfe nodded toward Serena—"because of a failed marriage in which he surely bore a substantial share of the responsibility.

"His anger often morphed into hatred and a desire to punish those to whom he bore strong animosities. Five persons in this room comprised the front rank of those he most detested, and he hit upon a devious plan to punish them."

"This sounds like pop psychology," Eric Haverhill scowled. "I still say that someone murdered Cameron."

"I briefly considered that Mr. Clay may indeed have been killed," Wolfe said, "but I could not conceive of any of those present carrying out the murder, or even having it done by proxy. Then, I got a report from Mr. Goodwin, who had attended Cameron Clay's funeral service. Something the minister said crystallized my thoughts. This pastor praised the deceased, using a well-known phrase. He said Mr. Clay 'comforted the afflicted and afflicted the comforted.'

"I do not know how much the columnist comforted the afflicted, but there is no doubt that he desired to afflict the comforted—in this case, those whom he detested, for a variety of reasons. So he devised the devious plan I alluded to moments ago."

"And just what was this so-called devious plan?" Haverhill demanded.

"Mr. Clay, with the help of Mr. McNeil here, worked to make a suicide appear to be a murder."

"Wait just a minute," Larry McNeil rasped, standing. "I—"

"Sit down and shut up!" Cramer bellowed. To Wolfe: "Go on."

"Thank you. Mr. Clay claimed he had been getting threatening telephone calls, and he told his superiors at the *Gazette* about this, naming the five individuals he felt could have been behind the calls. He suggested to them that he consult me, so I became an unwitting dupe in his plan. I am sad to say I took the bait."

"Enough with the self-flagellation," Cramer snapped. "Get on with it."

"From the start, the story of the telephone calls seemed questionable, as there was no one's word but Mr. Clay's that they ever transpired, other than Mr. McNeil's claim that he was present when Mr. Clay fielded one of them. Thus, the columnist would appear to have had a 'witness' to a threatening call, thereby establishing their credibility. Why would Mr. McNeil make up such a story?"

"So there were no calls?" Cordwell said, eyebrows raised.

"Never," Wolfe said, "but again, who would doubt Mr. Clay and his assistant? And given the vitriol many of his columns contained, it was hardly a stretch that he would receive threats. As a result, knowing his life was nearing its end and not wanting to suffer through the last stages of a ravaging illness, he decided to end his own life, but to make it seem like murder so that one of those he most detested would be accused and perhaps convicted. He may not have cared which of them bore the blame."

"So he shot himself?" Lon Cohen said.

"Yes, sir," Wolfe replied. "Because on numerous occasions he had spoken highly of Mr. McNeil's work as his assistant, I am sure he wanted the young man to continue his column, and he wanted to shield him from any suspicion in his apparent murder.

"Accordingly, the two of them planned the shooting to take place on a night when Mr. McNeil was at a gathering where several people could vouch for him. That immediately eliminated the young man as a suspect. The alibi was, as you like to say, Mr. Cramer, ironclad.

"Then to further make his death appear to be a murder, Mr. Clay left his front door ajar, suggesting that the 'murderer' somehow gained entry to the townhouse. As a plan, it was demoniacal, although Inspector Cramer never wavered in his insistence that this was a suicide."

"I have a hell of a lot of trouble believing this, Mr. Wolfe," Haverhill said. "I am still convinced that—" The owner of the *Gazette* was cut short by weeping that was coming from Larry McNeil.

"I . . . would have done . . . anything for Cameron. . . . Anything at all," McNeil said between sobs. "He was wonderful to me. When he first learned about the cancer and how far along it was, he told me he had an idea. When he first said the word *suicide*, I did everything I could to talk him out of it. 'You can beat this,' I told him. 'You're tough.'

"But he said the doctors had given him no hope at all, and that they would see that he got drugs that could ease the pain," McNeil went on, his sobs turning to wailing. "'Look, I know a way I can go out in a blaze of glory,' Cameron said to me, 'and with a little luck, I might be able to take somebody else with me.'"

There were gasps from the assemblage and a four-letter word shouted by Tobin. Cramer looked down at McNeil with a look of utter disgust. "How can you stand to live with yourself?" he said.

"I didn't want to do any of it," he moaned. "But Cameron . . . He was so excited by the idea. I resisted him on this for days, weeks, actually. But he wore me down. In the end, I couldn't say no to him."

"Didn't it bother you that someone else might get unfairly charged, Larry?" Ashton Cordwell asked.

McNeil nodded, wiping the tears from his face. "Yeah, I had a lot of trouble with that. But I also had a lot of trouble knowing that Cameron was going to shoot himself, and that he would be all alone when it happened."

"You could have stopped the whole damn thing right in its tracks," Cramer said.

"But Cameron kept telling me over and over that he couldn't stand the idea of a slow death. And I was the closest person to him; he had nobody else, nobody at all."

"You told Mr. Goodwin that he left the bulk of his money to the Salvation Army," Wolfe said.

"He did. The Salvation Army had helped his uncle in his last days, and Cameron never forgot that. It was just about the only organization that I ever heard him say anything good about."

"That bit of sentiment notwithstanding, we're seeing that Cameron Clay was a louse to the very end," Kerwin Andrews said. "They tell us not to speak ill of the dead, but I think an exception can be made here."

Millard Beardsley nodded vigorously. "I second that. The Lord tells us we will all be forgiven some day, but some people are beyond forgiveness, and I truly believe that Cameron Clay was one of them."

"Now just wait a minute," Eric Haverhill said angrily. "Cameron exposed a lot of wrongs in this city, and I was proud of the *Gazette* for carrying his column for all those years. He was a man of the people, a defender of the little guy."

"Defender mainly of himself," Roswell Stokes countered. "I know this fellow abetted the man's warped scheme, but I honestly believe that Clay had him under some kind of spell."

"That may be the case," Cramer said, "but nonetheless, we're going to be taking him in." The inspector then read McNeil his rights, and he and Purley Stebbins escorted him out of the office.

"What will happen to the young man?" Serena Sanchez asked. "Will he go to prison?"

"Probably not," Roswell Stokes said, "depending on who he gets to defend him."

"Mr. Wolfe, you have earned your fee," Ashton Cordwell said. "When you send me a bill, please include any expenses."

"Yeah, you did earn it," Eric Haverhill conceded. "You said early on that you might not find a murderer, and you were right. Did you have suspicions of this from the beginning?"

"I had inklings that the situation was not entirely what it seemed," Wolfe said, draining the last of his second beer.

CHAPTER 32

Inklings, huh?" I said to Wolfe after everyone had left. "Did you really have some?"

"I did. For one thing, none of the five people Clay had suggested as possible threats had what I felt was sufficient reason to kill him or to have him killed. Overall, they were not a likable bunch, but lack of likability is not necessarily an indication of an intent to kill."

"So you—" I was interrupted by the doorbell. "Maybe that's Cordwell, coming back to give you a check," I said, rising and heading down the hall. Through the glass, I saw the figure of Inspector Cramer.

"I hope I'm not calling too late, Archie," he said with unaccustomed politeness as I let him in. He almost never calls me by my first name.

"You're not. Mr. Wolfe and I were reviewing the events of the day," I told him as we headed for the office.

Wolfe did not seem surprised to see the inspector. "Will you have something to drink?" he asked. "I'm about to have more beer."

"I'll have a bourbon and water on the rocks," he said. I served the inspector first, then went to the kitchen for Wolfe's beer, knowing Fritz had turned in.

"That was quite a performance you put on tonight," Cramer said, when I returned, raising his glass in a salute. "I thought for sure you were going to tag someone with Clay's death."

Wolfe looked pleased. "Mr. Clay was something of a scoundrel, to say the least. He raised hatred to new levels."

"Yeah, that's hard to argue with," Cramer said. "To be charitable to the guy, I suppose you could say he did some good by blowing the whistle on some of the scum in this town. But he was a vicious bastard, and he didn't care who he hurt. Do you have any thoughts about which of those five Clay hoped would get nailed for his so-called murder?"

"He, of course, disliked all of them, but for different reasons. But I got the sense his repugnance toward Mr. Tobin was the strongest."

"That's where my repugnance lies, too," the inspector said with feeling. "The damage Tobin did to the department's reputation is going to hang around for a long time to come."

"No doubt. I presume Mr. McNeil will be charged."

"That's up to the DA, but I'd be surprised if he went to trial. You know as well as I do that when a newspaper is directly involved in a big story in this town, there's a lot of pressure to keep its bosses happy."

"Yes, the power of the press is not to be underestimated. You certainly have felt that power over the years."

"I have," Cramer said. "At one time or another, the editorial writers of at least four papers have called for my scalp, the *Gazette* among them."

"Yet you've survived all their shots," I put in.

"So far. But I figure that someday, one of those shots from the press is going to hit home with my bosses, and I'll be asked to turn in my badge. Maybe when that happens, you'll take me on as one of your part-time operatives, working alongside Panzer and Durkin."

I couldn't tell if the inspector was kidding, but the look on Wolfe's face was priceless. It's the closest I've ever seen to him registering shock.

The two old warhorses, who had butted heads so often over the years, went on talking and reminiscing for another half hour about cases they had been involved in and had fought about. I suspect the inspector's mellow mood had something to do with four words Wolfe had spoken earlier in the evening: "Inspector Cramer is correct." Cramer wasn't used to hearing that from Wolfe. I wondered how long this era of good feeling between them would continue. Probably until the next case we had, but for now, I leaned back with my scotch and enjoyed the moment.

CHAPTER 33

Larry McNeil got charged with interfering with a police investigation and abetting a suicide and was indicted. Ironically, he hired none other than Roswell Stokes to defend him, although I was not surprised, as Stokes had seemed sympathetic toward McNeil when everyone was gathered in the office. From the start, the trial was a circus, covered by all the local newspapers and TV and radio stations, as well as the Associated Press and the United Press International.

Stokes relished the exposure and rose to new heights of histrionics as he implored the jury to spare his youthful client. Things were slow in the brownstone one late March morning, so I decided to take in the trial, getting to the courthouse early because of Lon Cohen's advice. "They're packing the place every day, Archie, so you may not get a seat, and I can't give you press credentials," Lon said. "They've all been gobbled up."

I got in, all right, and I saw a sample of vintage Stokes in action. "This young man, as loyal an assistant as anyone could ever ask for, found himself in a terrible position," the lanky lawyer said, loping back and forth in front of the jury box and brushing a shock of hair from his eye in what had to be a practiced gesture.

"Put yourselves in my client's place, ladies and gentlemen," Stokes went on. "His respected mentor is dying of a terminal illness. There is no hope whatever of recovery. Cameron Clay has decided to end his own life, but in so doing, he also wishes to exact revenge upon any one of several people he feels deserve punishment—me among them." That evoked gasps from some jurors.

"Yes, you heard right—*me among them*. And so, ladies and gentlemen, you must be asking yourselves at this moment: Why am I defending this young man, whose mentor detested me to the point that he was willing to make me, along with four other persons, seem to be a suspect in his murder? I will tell you why I am defending Mr. McNeil: Because he is an honorable man who was placed in an untenable position. He was asked to be a party to a suicide, the suicide of a man he revered and loyally served. But it would be a suicide to prevent the agonies that were surely to come.

"Is there any one among you who has had to watch a loved one die slowly? How many of you have wished you could speed that person's death to spare the agonizing pain he or she was going through? I did, when my father was dying of a brain tumor. His own pain was horrible, and had I been stronger, I would have helped him to end his life. To this day, I am sorry that I did nothing to ease his unutterable pain."

That speech of Stokes was surely what got Larry McNeil off, although all the way through the trial, the prosecution argued that Stokes had a conflict of interest in the case. "I see no conflict of interest here," the judge said to the assistant district attorney. "If anything, one might assume that Mr. Stokes would resent the defendant for his part in attempting to besmirch him. Objection overruled."

Objection overruled became the byword of the trial as, time and again, the prosecution attacked Stokes and his methods, only to be rebuffed from the bench. When the jury after a short deliberation returned a verdict of innocent for Larry McNeil, there was applause and cheering in the courtroom.

McNeil did not inherit the column Cameron Clay had written for so many years—no one did. As Lon Cohen told me later, "Both Cordwell and Haverhill felt he was still too green to get a high-visibility column like that, although they've kept him on the staff as a feature writer, and he has done some damn good human-interest stuff. If I were to guess, I'd say that after a couple of more years, he just may end up getting a column like Clay's after all. So all in all, things have worked out well for him."

For the other principals in the Cameron Clay case, it was a mixed bag. Roswell Stokes burnished his flamboyant reputation by his impassioned defense of Larry McNeil, and if anything, because of the case's publicity, he now seems to be in even greater demand as a defense attorney. How Clay would have hated that.

Kerwin Andrews suffered a crushing rebuke when the city's building and zoning officials rejected his plans for his ambitious Andrews Point project. Part of their concern was the shoddy construction work that had been done on several of his earlier projects. In addition, however, the developer had been up to his old tricks of trying to bribe his way to success, and he got caught when a high-principled zoning inspector reported him.

As the *Gazette*'s editorial about the event, headlined CASTLES IN THE SAND, read: "This setback, for all intents and purposes, brings an end to the meteoric career of Kerwin Andrews. In all likelihood, the once high-riding developer will never again be able to enlist the backers necessary to fund his grandiose projects. Of more pressing concern to Mr. Andrews is avoiding indictment. Here is a cautionary tale of a man's boundless—and reckless—ambition."

Millard Beardsley recently won yet another term as a councilman. For the first time, he had a serious challenger, a youthful reformer who promised to represent the district with "honor, dignity, and a crusading fervor." Early newspaper polls had the challenger running ahead, but these polls apparently focused too heavily on the more youthful and disaffected members of the electorate. When Election Day came, Beardsley was swept in by a comfortable margin, claiming that "when push comes to shove, the people know who can do the most for them. I humbly accept their affirmation."

Michael Tobin, the disgraced former cop, only outlived his nemesis Cameron Clay by a few months. Tobin had a fatal heart attack, and his body was found on the floor of the florist shop in Yonkers where I had met him and persuaded him to meet with Nero Wolfe.

"That newspaper columnist killed him!" Tobin's tearful widow told a TV reporter. "Just as sure as he had taken a gun and shot him. Mike was a broken man. What a sorry way New York City has treated one of its most hardworking and loyal servants."

As I was going through the Sunday *Times* society section the other day, I came across an item on the weddings pages that brought me up short. The headline read THE BANKER TAKES HIMSELF A DIVA, and the photograph showed a beaming Serena Sanchez wearing a long gown and a tiara standing beside a tall, white-haired swell whose smile was every bit as wide as her own. The caption: "Edgar Baxter Harrison IV, chairman of the Continental Trust Company, and the opera singer Serena Sanchez at the reception following their wedding on the grounds of The Breakers in Newport, Rhode Island." The accompanying article chronicled the "whirlwind romance" that followed their having met at a Metropolitan Opera party.

I put down the paper and telephoned Lily Rowan. "I ran across an interesting item in today's *Times*," I told her.

"Is that right? Whatever was it about?"

"I believe you can guess."

She laughed. "Did it by any chance have to do with a mutual acquaintance of ours?"

"Good guess. Have you known about this for a while?"

"Not all that long. I just finished reading the same article you did, and the *Times* described the courtship accurately. This was really a whirlwind romance, just a few weeks."

"I hope it turns out better than a previous marriage, which as I recall also resulted from a chance meeting at a Met party."

"I hope so, too," Lily said. "I happen to know Ed Harrison fairly well, and he is a fine man, a real gentleman, a word you could never apply to Cameron Clay."

"True."

"I probably shouldn't tell you this, given that you're pretty darned pleased with yourself . . ."

"I'm not sure how to take that comment, but now that you've started, what are you about to tell me?"

"A few days after that weekend up in Katonah, I ran into Serena at a luncheon. She told me what a good time she had, and she told me something else."

"Am I going to have to drag it out of you?"

Another laugh. "She told me, 'I must say, I am very taken with your Archie Goodwin. If he were the beau of anyone but you, I would do everything I could to get him.' Now just what do you think of that, Mr. Goodwin?"

"I think the lady has shown extremely good taste. However, I have good taste as well, which is why I would never consider having a relationship with her, given the far superior relationship I already have."

"That comment does prove that you are pleased with yourself, Escamillo, and it also proves that you do indeed have good taste. But then, so do I."

AUTHOR'S NOTE

This tale is set in the late 1970s, and all of its characters are fictional. The only historical figures mentioned in the narrative are the longtime gossip columnist Walter Winchell (1923–1972) and the famed and mercurial opera diva Maria Callas (1923–1977).

At the height of Winchell's popularity, his syndicated column appeared in two thousand newspapers worldwide and was read daily by as many as fifty million people. His Sunday night radio program, which ran from the 1930s to the 1950s, had an audience of twenty million.

The fiery soprano Maria Callas was arguably the most famous diva of the mid-century period. American-born of Greek parents, she received her musical education in Greece, but her career began to flourish in Italy. Famed for both her talent and her temperament, she had a tumultuous personal life that included a well-publicized affair with Greek shipping tycoon Aristotle Onassis.

The Apollo Theater on 125th Street, which Archie noted on his visit to Councilman Millard Beardsley's office, has been a fixture in New York's Harlem neighborhood for more than a century. Begun as a burlesque house, the theater later switched to vaudeville acts and big bands, and eventually concentrated on African-American performers and acts.

The *New York Gazette*, frequently mentioned in Rex Stout's stories over the years, is a fictitious daily newspaper. The other New York papers cited in the story, the *Times*, the *Daily News*, and the *Post*, are, of course, actual dailies, and all are still being published.

As with my previous Nero Wolfe novels, I want to acknowledge Barbara Stout and Rebecca Stout Bradbury for their continuing support and encouragement. My thanks also go to my agent, Martha Kaplan; to Otto Penzler and Rob Hart of Mysterious Press; and to the fine team at Open Road Integrated Media.

My warmest thanks of all go to my wife, Janet, who has been an unfailing source of support for more than half a century. What a ride we have had!

ABOUT THE AUTHOR

Robert Goldsborough is an American author best known for continuing Rex Stout's famous Nero Wolfe series. Born in Chicago, he attended Northwestern University and upon graduation went to work for the Associated Press, beginning a lifelong career in journalism that would include long periods at the *Chicago Tribune* and *Advertising Age*.

While at the *Tribune*, Goldsborough began writing mysteries in the voice of Rex Stout, the creator of iconic sleuths Nero Wolfe and Archie Goodwin. Goldsborough's first novel starring Wolfe, *Murder in E Minor* (1986), was met with acclaim from both critics and devoted fans, winning a Nero Award from the Wolfe Pack. Ten more Wolfe mysteries followed, including *Death on Deadline* (1987) and *Fade to Black* (1990). In 2005, Goldsborough published *Three Strikes You're Dead*, the first in an original series starring *Chicago Tribune* reporter Snap Malek. *Stop the Presses!* (2016) is his most recent novel.

THE NERO WOLFE MYSTERIES

FROM MYSTERIOUSPRESS.COM
AND OPEN ROAD MEDIA

MYSTERIOUSPRESS.COM

MYSTERIOUSPRESS.COM

Otto Penzler, owner of the Mysterious Bookshop in Manhattan, founded the Mysterious Press in 1975. Penzler quickly became known for his outstanding selection of mystery, crime, and suspense books, both from his imprint and in his store. The imprint was devoted to printing the best books in these genres, using fine paper and top dust-jacket artists, as well as offering many limited, signed editions.

Now the Mysterious Press has gone digital, publishing ebooks through **MysteriousPress.com**.

MysteriousPress.com offers readers essential noir and suspense fiction, hard-boiled crime novels, and the latest thrillers from both debut authors and mystery masters. Discover classics and new voices, all from one legendary source.